…CGHT!

Zach resumed circling. If he could get the drop on them, he'd free Frazier. Once on the run, he would use all the tricks he'd learned from his father and his Shoshone friends to elude the cutthroats.

"I'm tired of you pestering me," Kendrick was saying. "So if you want equal shares for your brother and you, scat. Or the rest of us will divide it up five ways."

Five! Kendrick had said five! Zach remembered seeing that many near the old trapper earlier but now there were only four, plus Billy. One of them had disappeared while Lou and he were riding down the ridge. But where to?

The answer came in the form of a distinct metallic click as a gun muzzle was jammed against his temple.

WILDERNESS

Gold Rage

David Thompson

LEISURE BOOKS NEW YORK CITY

To Judy, Joshua, and Shane.

A LEISURE BOOK®

May 1999

Published by

Dorchester Publishing Co., Inc.
276 Fifth Avenue
New York, NY 10001

ISBN 0-8439-4519-2

Gold Rage

Chapter One

Ben Frazier squinted at the blazing sun, then wiped a grimy sleeve across his sweating brow. "I reckon it's about time, Bessy."

The old man said it sadly. He had been in the mountains a long time. One of the first to see the potential in the beaver trade, he had arrived in the Rockies with the first company of free trappers. That had been decades earlier. His plan had been to make enough from raising plews to set himself up comfortably for life. During idle moments, he'd daydreamed of becoming as fabulously wealthy as John Jacob Astor.

But things never quite work out like a person figures. Raising plews was a lot harder than Frazier had counted on. Truth was, trapping was god-awful hard work. The toil, the cold water, took a fearsome toll on a body's health. And there were other perilous factors to deal with. Savage beasts that would as soon eat a man as look at him. Equally savage warriors who took a dim view of having their territories invaded by whites. All in all, the life of a trapper wasn't for the squeamish.

Frazier persevered, even though he'd never gotten rich. Oh, he'd had nine or ten really good years where he earned a couple of thousand dollars, and this in a day and age when the average worker was lucky if he brought home four hundred annually.

If Frazier had been smart and saved some, he could have gone back to the States with a tidy nest egg. But he'd fallen into the same rut most trappers did. At each summer's rendezvous he received payment for the peltries he'd collected, and before each rendezvous was over, he had always spent most of his earnings.

Only part of the blame could be placed on greedy traders and company men who milked the trappers for every cent that could be squeezed from their possibles bags. It always angered Frazier to think that in St. Louis sugar cost ten cents a pound but at the rendezvous it went for two dollars. Lead for bullets went for six cents a pound back in the United States. Come rendezvous time, it went for up to three dollars. And so on and so forth.

Prices for goods were outrageous, but the truth was that most mountain men could restock all the provisions they'd need for a few hundred dollars. So where did the rest of the money they earned go? Where did money *always* go? It was spent on women, whiskey, and gambling.

Frazier was no different from his friends. Once he bought enough supplies, he'd spend up to two weeks in fearsome debauchery. Drinking until he passed out night after night. Frolicking with willing maidens who swapped their charms for expensive geegaws. Literally throwing his money away by betting on horse races and wrestling matches and shooting contests.

Small wonder, then, that by the end of each rendezvous Frazier was usually as broke as he was when he arrived. Small wonder he never saved a nickel. Small wonder that when beaver fur fell out of fashion back east and the trapping trade dried up, Ben was left with barely a hundred dollars to his name and a mule as contrary as the grass was green.

Now the annual rendezvous was no more. The trapping fraternity had disbanded. Most had headed back to the States. Ben had almost done the same, although it galled him to slink off with his tail between his legs, like a whipped cur. He'd had such a *grand* dream.

Then the Almighty sent a godsend in the form of a friendly Arapaho by the name of White Antelope. They had met many winters before when a much younger Frazier stumbled on a small Arapaho village. Wariness had grown into guarded respect and eventual friendship. On many an occasion Frazier had stayed at White Antelope's lodge, always bringing presents for the family. It got so, the children called him "Uncle."

About two months ago, on a pleasantly cool evening, as Frazier sat glumly beside a crackling fire, pondering how unfair life was, he'd been alarmed to hear the light tread of a footstep. Leaping up, he'd brought his heavy Hawken to bear, then relaxed when out of the shadows stepped White Antelope.

The warrior had heard about the collapse of the beaver trade and had come to say good-bye. The gesture mightily touched Frazier. As a token of affection, he gave White Antelope a spare Green River knife, a fine blade, never used. The Arapaho had admired it awhile, then taken a small pouch from his side.

"I have something for you, as well, Scared of Rabbits."

Frazier thought back to that morning, shortly after they met, when a rabbit had bounded from some brush and startled him so badly, he'd jumped and accidentally snapped off a shot. The Arapahos thought his antics hilarious. Thus, the name. "There is no need to give me anything. You have shared your lodge and your food more times than I can count. The knife is my small way of saying thanks."

"One gift deserves another," White Antelope replied. He'd held the pouch in his palm. "I know how much whites value that which you call 'money.' I also know you have little of it, and that you would like to have much."

The reminder soured Frazier. "My people breathe money."

"I do not understand."

"Think of it this way. The worth of an Arapaho warrior is measured by how many coup he has counted and how many horses he owns. The worth of a white man is measured by how much money he has and how many things he has bought with it." Frazier sighed and said in English, "It's why I've spent all those winters breakin' my back raisin' plews. Beaver hides were worth a heap of money for a spell."

"Why only beaver, my friend? A fox hide sheds water just as well. A bear hide is warmer. And the hide of a buffalo has many more uses."

"I know," Frazier said, reverting to Arapaho. "But the whites who live east of the Muddy River only wanted beaver. My people call that 'fashion.' "

"Again I do not understand."

"White people who have a lot of money like to buy a lot of clothes. But never the same kind of clothes for very long. For a while they liked beaver hats and beaver trim, but now they are bored with that and have gone on to something else. Silk, I heard it's called."

White Antelope had digested the information. "White people are strange. My people have worn buckskins for more winters than anyone can remember. Why should we change, when buckskin is easy for our women to cure and sew, and holds up so well?"

"There are days, my friend, when I almost wish I'd been born an Arapaho."

The warrior smiled. "Your words touch my heart, Scared of Rabbits. Here." He held out the pouch.

Thinking it must contain a few coins acquired in barter, Frazier had loosened the drawstring and upended the contents into his right hand. Bathed in the flickering glow of the firelight were a dozen kernel-size golden pebbles. Frazier looked closer, and gasped.

"Grizzly Killer once told me that white men value these yellow stones as much as they do money. I have no use for them. But I thought you might."

Flabbergasted, Frazier had taken a nugget and bitten it. "Gold!" he'd declared. "Good God in heaven, it's real gold!"

"They please you, then?"

In Arapaho, Frazier exclaimed, "Friend, you have given me the greatest gift any white man can possess! Where did you get these?"

"I found them."

"Are there any more where they came from?"

"As many as there are stars in the sky."

Frazier's mind had raced. "Did you have to dig very deep?"

"Dig?" The warrior snorted. "They were in a stream. So shiny and bright they caught my eye, so I picked some up. I did not know what they were." White Antelope paused. "I can show you where, if you would like."

And so Ben Frazier had been led to a stream high in the mountains, a stream too shallow and narrow to harbor beaver, a stream overlooked by all other mountaineers as being of no consequence. Little did they know. For it was just as White Antelope claimed. Nuggets were as plentiful as ripe grapes in a vineyard.

The warrior had gone off to rejoin his people, and for weeks afterward Frazier spent every waking moment gathering the gold up, enough to make him the richest man in all Creation. He filled parfleche after parfleche, making new ones from deer hide as the need arose.

Frazier wasn't a prospector. He didn't know a lot about minerals and geology. As near as he could gather, the nuggets and grains had been washed down from higher up, no doubt from a vein the likes of which would put old King Midas to shame. He tried a few times to find it, without success. Which didn't bother him at all, because he still had hundreds of pounds ready to take out. Unfortunately, he had no way to transport it. Bessy couldn't be expected to tote that much clear across the plains. What he needed were packhorses, five or six good, sturdy animals, and he knew just where to get his hands on some: Bent's Fort.

On this hot day in late summer, Ben Frazier mounted his mule and headed down the mountain. Gold Mountain, he'd named it, for an obvious reason. His treasure was safely cached except for two bulging pokes hidden under his beaded buckskin shirt. He would use them to buy the pack animals he needed and be on his way to the States within the week.

And that was why Frazier was sad. No more majestic Rockies. No more rugged peaks rearing to the clouds. No more towering ramparts crowned by mantles of glistening snow. No more eagles soaring on high, no elk bugling in the valleys. No more of the natural wonderland he had come to love so much.

Ben would miss the splendor, but he was looking forward to living the life of a country squire. He'd buy a big estate somewhere, with woods for hunting and a lake for fishing, and he'd spend his waning days in ease and luxury. Damn, it would be fine! He imagined riding in a plush carriage, imagined wearing whatever in hell was the latest in high-society fashion, imagined being the talk of the town, of having pretty ladies on his arm when he went to the theater and such.

To at last be rich, after all the toil and sweat and disappointment, was a heady experience. Ben rode with a song in his heart, his spirits soaring to the clouds. He resolved to make a list of all the things he'd always had a hankering for but could never afford so that once he was set up, he could treat himself.

"Bessy, life will be sweet. I'll eat off china plates

and drink from china cups. I'll have a gal to serve my food three times a day. And one of them fellers who opens doors and fetches tea. I'll wear a jacket with tails on it, and have one of those newfangled hats that look like a stovepipe.''

The mule ambled briskly on. It was used to his rambling.

''Yes, sir. The Almighty finally got around to givin' me what I deserve. I reckon I'll thank Him by donatin' some to a church. Doesn't hardly matter which one, since they all say they have His ear.''

For the rest of that day, Frazier cheerily envisioned the great and wonderful times in store for him. He stopped for the night in a gully that offered shelter from the wind, and where his fire was unlikely to be spotted by hostile eyes. His dreams were of mansions and lace. At first light he forked leather, bearing to the southeast. He whistled softly, the Hawken resting across his thighs.

Along about noon the acrid scent of smoke brought Frazier to a halt. Wispy gray tendrils in high pines to the east alerted him to the presence of a camp. White men or red, it was unimportant. He was determined to avoid contact with others as much as was possible until he reached St. Louis.

But then, as he swung to the right to give the pines a wide berth, two riders appeared, traveling in his general direction. They were whites, much younger than Frazier. Dressed in badly worn and faded homespun clothes, they had a haggard, weary aspect. From the pommel of one saddle hung a sack such as trappers used to carry traps and whatnot.

They didn't see Frazier, and probably would have gone on by if he hadn't hailed them. Why he changed his mind, Frazier couldn't say. Maybe it was the fact it had been months since he last jawed with a fellow citizen. Maybe it was his good mood. Maybe it was stupidity. Whatever the case, he helloed and rode into the open, saying, ''Howdy there, gents! It's good for these old eyes to see some young coons like your-selves! Have any 'bacca in your possibles?''

The two men had been taken utterly by surprise. A rodent-faced fellow, who favored a mackinaw coat two sizes too big, snickered and said, ''Well, lookee here, Billy. We done found us someone's grandpa.''

The other, who was barely old enough to shave, gestured sharply. ''Pay Ed Stark no mind, mister. He's always got a burr up his butt. I'm William Batson, but everyone just calls me Billy.''

Frazier introduced himself, then nodded at the smoke. ''You boys alone?''

''No, sir,'' Billy said. ''There's seven of us, bound for the States. Would you care to meet the others? You'd be more than welcome to light and sit a spell. We don't have any tobacco left, but there's coffee on.''

Ed Stark frowned. ''Kendrick sent us to find meat for the supper pot. He won't take it kindly if we return empty-handed.''

Billy stiffened. ''Oh. That's right.'' To Frazier he said, ''Sorry, mister. But we'd better do as Mr. Kendrick told us or he's liable to get riled. And I wouldn't want that.''

The old trapper thought it peculiar the two men would let someone boss them around, but it was their affair, not his. ''How about if I help?''

''We'd be obliged,'' Billy answered cheerfully. ''But we have to hurry. I need to get back as quick as I can.'' He didn't say why.

It took half an hour. Frazier flushed a buck, bringing it down with a single shot through the brainpan. Ed Stark hurriedly cut off a haunch, threw it over his shoulder heedless of the blood that oozed onto his clothes, and climbed back on his sorrel.

''What about the rest of the deer?'' Frazier asked.

''What about it?'' Stark rejoined. ''This here is enough to go around.''

''We can't dawdle,'' Billy stressed.

The two young men trotted off. Reluctantly, Frazier followed, saying softly to Bessy, "What an awful waste. Young'uns nowadays ain't got no common sense. Why, my pa would've taken a switch to me if I ever squandered meat like they do."

In a sizable clearing among stately pines lay their camp. Four grungy men were hunkered beside a fifth, who was on his back, covered by blankets to his chin. They regarded Frazier in a cold manner, as they might a rattler that had crawled into their midst. The biggest of the bunch, a strapping he-bear with shoulders wider than a grizzly's, was coldest of all. Frazier pegged him as their leader, Kendrick, and his hunch was proven right by the first words out of the big man's mouth.

"What the hell is this, Ed? I send you after supper and you bring back this mangy old coot?"

"This old coot can speak for himself," Frazier stated. "Seems to me, friend, your manners are plumb atrocious. In these parts a stranger is generally made welcome. Or don't you believe in being hospitable?"

Some of the others tensed and looked at Kendrick as if they expected him to cut loose with his rifle or pistols, but the big man merely said, "I'll be dogged. We've got us a regular hellion. Sure, mister, I believe in being hospitable. It's just that we're a mite peeved at your kind right now. Don't hold it against us, though."

"My kind?" Frazier said, puzzled.

"You're a trapper, ain't you?"

"I was. So?"

"So it's all the old farts like you who've killed off all the beaver," Kendrick said testily. "You see, my partners and me came all the way west to become trappers. All those weeks crossing the prairie, all those days of terrible heat and thirst and going without food. And what did we find when we got here? That pretty near all the damn beaver have been trapped out. Ain't hardly enough left to make a decent coat."

The accusation shocked Frazier. "Now, hold on.

It's not my fault the bottom fell out of the beaver market.''

"True," Kendrick agreed. "Between the time we left our homes over a year ago, and the last rendezvous, it surely did. But by then we'd gotten here. By then we'd learned the hard way that most of the beaver were already gone. Thanks to you and those like you.''

Billy Batson fidgeted in his saddle. "It doesn't hardly seem fair to blame this one fellow, Mr. Kendrick. I mean, he's only one man, and there have been hundreds working the streams and rivers hereabouts for years.''

Kendrick sniffed. "I suppose you have a point. Climb on down, stranger. Make yourself comfortable. No hard feelings, I hope.''

Frazier had half a mind to tell the big man to go to hell, and leave. But the aroma of freshly brewed coffee reminded him that he had run out months before and would dearly love a cup. "None at all. Livin' in the wild tends to make folks a big tetchy.''

All seven were young, none over twenty-five. Kendrick appeared to be the oldest, although the man under the blankets was approximately the same age. His pasty face beaded with perspiration, the man shivered and shook as if he were instead covered by snow and ice.

"What's ailin' him?" Frazier inquired.

"Fever," Kendrick said. "He came down with it two days ago, and we've been waiting for it to break so we can go on.''

Billy dismounted and knelt next to their stricken companion. "This here is Frank, my older brother. Him and me were brought up on a farm in Ohio, but we got tired of walking behind a plow all day. When we saw a notice that Mr. Kendrick was starting up his own trapping brigade, we joined right away. Thought it would make us rich.'' He laughed bitterly.

Frazier knew the booshways—the leaders of trapping parties—by sight. At one time or another he had met every one. At *no* time had he ever set eyes on Kendrick. Which told him the man was a fool. Kendrick had taken it into his head to lead a brigade without having any idea what it entailed—without ever having trapped. Based solely on tales and rumor, the idiot had led gullible greeners on a trek that might well have gotten them killed. His opinion of the big man dropped several more notches.

A short, pudgy gent stepped foward. "The handle is Cyrus Walton, from Titusfield, the corncob capital of the world. Maybe you've heard of it?"

Frazier had to admit he never had. He was introduced to the last two, an ungainly scarecrow called Ira Sanders and a bristle-bearded walking barrel who went by the name of Elden Johnson. Bobbing his chin at each, Frazier turned and squatted beside Frank Batson. The former farmer's brow was as hot as a red ember. "This jasper needs doctorin'," he commented.

"Think we don't know that?" Ed Stark snapped. "But none of us know much about medicine."

Frazier doubted they knew much about *anything,* but he held his tongue and climbed back on Bessy. "There are some roots that might help. The Arapaho use them all the time."

Kendrick was skeptical. "An Indian remedy? You've been up in these mountains too long, old man. All that red mumbo jumbo doesn't amount to a hill of beans."

"Shows how bright you are," Frazier couldn't resist responding. "Indians have forgotten more about treatin' ailments than the white man will ever learn. I've seen them cure everything from a toothache to a crippled leg."

Ed Stark's ferret features curled in a scowl. "Sounds to me as if we've got us one of them Injun-lovers on our hands, boys. I'll bet this old coon has even lived with the heathens."

"What if I have?" Frazier said. He'd had enough of their attitude. He would forget the coffee and light a shuck as soon as he tended Frank Batson. "I'll be back directly with what you need," he told Billy, then departed.

The roots were not difficult to find. They came from a flowery plant known to some tribes as *poku sinop*. Within an hour he was approaching the camp again, enough roots in his parfleche to do the job.

Billy anxiously awaited him. "I sure hope you can help Frank. His fever is getting worse."

That it was. The old trapper filled his coffeepot with water from a water skin belonging to the scarecrow, Sanders. He crushed the *poku sinop,* added two handfuls, and stirred until the concoction boiled. Some of the younger men watched with interest, but not Kendrick and Stark. They stood aloof, resentment mirrored in their eyes.

Frazier had met sour sorts like those two before. The kind who blamed everyone else for their own shortcomings. That they held him to blame for the decline in the beaver trade was outrageous, but typical. Sure, he had collected more peltries than most, but he had hardly single-handedly driven the beaver to near extinction.

If anyone or anything was close to extinct, it was the trappers themselves. Only the Hudson's Bay Company had any men in the field, and most were well to the north and west. The few free trappers still around were turning to varied pursuits to make ends meet. A few were guiding pilgrims along the Oregon Trail. Some had become scouts for the Army. Still others had gone east to end out their days in rocking chairs.

Hot drops suddenly seared Frazier's wrist. Jerking his hand back, he blew on it, then carefully filled a tin cup with tea. Everyone gathered around as he stepped to Frank Batson, who was tossing and turning. "Hold him down," Ben directed Billy.

The younger sibling hastened to comply. "Be still, Frank. This gentleman is trying to help."

Frank didn't reply. Eyelids fluttering, his whole body quaking, he groaned loudly.

Frazier placed the cup down, then gently lifted the sick man's head onto his leg. It would take five or six cups, but by morning the fever should show signs of breaking and in twenty-four hours the Ohioan would be weak but well. "Open your mouth," he said, pulling at Frank's lower jaw, which grew slack. Frazier quickly picked up the cup and tilted it so some of the medicine trickled down Batson's throat.

Abruptly, Frank sputtered and coughed and lurched upward. Dazed, gaping in confusion, he clutched at the old trapper. "What's going on? Who are you?"

Billy put a hand on his brother's arm "You're sickly, Franklyn. Don't you remember?"

"I'm trying to help," Frazier said, and went to push Batson back down. But the former farmer resisted, delirium lending him exceptional strength. "Please calm yourself. I only want to get some medicine into you."

Frank muttered incoherently and struggled to rise.

"I could use some help here," Frazier declared. He made the request too late. Batson tore at him, attempting to heave him aside, and in so doing wrenched Frazier's buckskin shirt above his belt. One of the pouches fell, thudding at Kendrick's feet, and some of the nuggets spilled out.

Except for Frank Batson, everyone froze. Every gaze locked on the nuggets. Kendrick slowly bent and selected the largest. "Is this what I think it is?" he asked no one in particular.

Ed Stark snatched up the pouch. "Gold! The whole damn thing is filled with gold!" He waved it at the others as if it were the Holy Grail. "There must be hundreds of dollars' worth!"

"All mine," Frazier growled. Giving the tin cup to Billy, he extended an arm. "I'll thank you to hand it over."

"Not so fast," Kendrick said. He glanced at Ira

Sanders and Elden Johnson and barked, "Hold him, boys!"

Frazier stabbed for a pistol, but they were on him before he could straighten and unlimber either flintlock. Iron fingers held him fast. Billy Batson protested, to no avail. Kendrick, smirking, patted Frazier's sides. His smirk widening, the big man reached under Frazier's shirt and pulled out the second pouch.

"I thought so. And something tells me you know where there's a lot more."

"Maybe I do," Frazier blundered, and realized it the moment he spoke. "But I'll never tell you."

A butcher knife blossomed in Kendrick's other hand as if out of the rarefied air. "Reckon so, do you, old man?" He leaned forward. "I think you will."

Chapter Two

They were young and they were in love. And when two people are in heaven, the whole world seems heavenly.

Louisa May Clark certainly thought so. To her, the sky was bluer than it had ever been, the grass was greener, the trees were loftier. The Rockies had a fresh-scrubbed look about them, as if an invisible giant had spruced them up just for her. Every mighty peak pulsed with renewed vitality, the same renewed vitality that pumped through her own veins.

Who could blame her for being so happy? Not long before she had lost her father, when he was brutally slain by hostiles. Before that, her mother. Louisa had been left alone in the middle of the vast wilderness, an orphan adrift in the dangerous sea of life. Her prospects for survival, let alone happiness, had been nil.

Then Louisa met Zachary King. His dislike of whites and her dislike of Indians had resulted in mutual spite at first. But the longer they were together, the more they learned about each other, the better they understood each other, the closer they grew. Never in her wildest imaginings would Louisa have thought she could fall for someone like him. Yet she had. And now, thanks to their chance meeting, she had discovered bliss of an order she never suspected existed.

Louisa was in *love*! Heart and soul, she adored Zach King. Or Stalking Coyote, as he was known to the Shoshones. Long before, the tribe had adopted the King family, in large part because Nate King, Zach's father, had taken a Shoshone woman as his wife. In fact, Zach had spent so much time among them, he could pass for a full-blooded Shoshone warrior.

Who would have thought, Louisa mused, that she would ever love someone who was part Indian?

Life was so strange. After her pa died, Louisa had been in the darkest depths of despair. Now she was giddy with rapture, and thrilled to be alive.

Where before the Rockies had seemed rife with menace and every shadow hid a potential threat, now the mountains were paradise on Earth. Her love had magically transformed them, just as it had magically transformed her, softening her hardened heart and letting her see everything in a whole new light.

Louisa finally understood why poets and the like were forever spouting on about *love, love, love.* She understood why they claimed it was the answer to all the world's woes. For if everyone could only learn to love one another, the evils of the world would melt away like wax under a hot sun.

From the fountain of love gushed well-being and joy. At least, this was true in Louisa's case, and she figured it was the same for everybody. Now, glancing at the handsome object of her monumental affection, she said softly for the umpteenth time that day, "I love you."

Zach King responded automatically. "I love you, too." But he meant it, meant every syllable. The young woman beside him—let no one *dare* call her a girl even if she was not quite seventeen yet—meant everything to him. There was nothing he wouldn't do for her. No challenge he wouldn't meet. Her every wish was his command.

At times Zach felt silly feeling as he did. He was acting the same as lovestruck Shoshone friends of his, young men his age who had undergone the same remarkable change. One day, they were interested in horses and tales of battle and counting coup; the next, they were interested only in the maidens of their dreams, and would dote on them to the exclusion of all else.

Yes, it was silly. Yet it could not be helped. Zach's father had been right, as he usually was. Years ago, on a blustery winter's night when the wind howled outside their warm cabin and snow lashed the roof, they had talked about matters of love and intimacy. Nate answered a hundred questions Zach posed. And during the course of their talk, his father said something Zach never forgot: "Don't fret, son. When the time comes, you'll know it. You have no interest in girls right now except as playmates, and that's as it should be. But there will come a day when you'll change. When something inside of you will flare up like the wick on a lantern when it's lit. And nothing you can do can stop it from happening."

Zach was glad his pa's prediction had turned out to be true.

Now, lightly clasping the reins to his dun, Zachary admired Lou without being obvious. She had on new beaded buckskins, courtesy of Winona, his mother, who had taught Lou how to make them. They clung to Lou's lithe form like a second skin. Her eyes sparkled, her chin was held proudly high.

It pleased Zach that she had started to let her brown hair grow. Previously, it had been cropped short so her father could pass her off as a boy and avoid unwanted attention in a land where white women were as scarce as hawk's teeth. All in all, where Zach was concerned, Louisa May Clark was the perfect vision of feminine loveliness.

Unknown to him, Louisa was doing the same thing he was. She admired his high cheekbones and the width of his shoulders. With his long black hair and bronzed features, Zach was as fine a figure of a man as any who ever lived, in Lou's estimation.

His buckskins, his moccasins, had been fashioned Shoshone-style. Around his waist, as around hers, were two pistols and a knife. Both were armed with Hawkens, both had ammo pouches and powder horns crisscrossing their chests, and Zach also had a possibles bag, typical of most mountain men.

Lordy, but he is good-looking! Lou marveled. In her whimsy she compared him to the great heroes she had heard about when she was little, to the likes of Jason and Hercules, to famed King Arthur and fearless Sir Lancelot, and found them all wanting. Zach was handsomer, stronger, more manly. And he was *hers*.

The shriek of an eagle drew Louisa's gaze to a soaring silhouette far overhead. They were well to the west of the King cabin and had been on the go for two days. Another two and they would stop at a place Zach knew of, a high basin—or park, as the trappers called them—which they would have all to themselves for as long as they desired to stay. She couldn't wait.

The jaunt had not been their idea. Amazingly, Winona King had come up with it at supper a week ago. "I think the two of you should get away for a little while," she had said out of the blue. "Go off and enjoy yourselves."

But had it been out of the blue? Lou now wondered.

Zach and she had been flitting about like hummingbirds ever since Zach proposed. Naturally, she had said yes, and the two of them had been all set to start living together then and there. But Zach's parents had laid down a condition: They must wait a year. By then Zach would be almost nineteen and she would be seventeen. They could have a formal Shoshone celebration, with all of Winona's kin involved, and begin their new life "proper," as Nate King put it.

Initially, Louisa had been upset. She'd much rather become Zach's wife right away. But the more she thought about it, the more she realized it made sense. It would give them time to get to know one another better, and to plan to meet the demands their new life would impose. So many questions had to be settled. Where would they live? In the same valley as Nate and Winona? In a valley of their own? Or with the Shoshones? What would Zach do once they were man and wife? How would he help support them? What should *she* do to contribute her fair share?

They had been trying to work it out. Oh, *how* they'd been trying. Day after day they had debated what was best, and it had stunned Lou to find that often Zach's ideas were completely the opposite of her own. So they hashed them out, and hashed them out some more, to the point where they started to get on each other's nerves and were sniping at each other as if they were already married.

Louisa suddenly laughed aloud. So *that* was the reason Winona King had advised them to spend some time alone!

"What's so funny?" Zach asked while threading his dun through aspens toward a jagged ridge above.

"I was just thinking," Lou answered. Bending, she reached over and brushed his hand with her own, careful not to swerve her mare too close to his mount. "You know, I've never been happier in all my born days."

"Makes two of us."

"Honestly and truly?"

"Truly and honestly."

It was a private ritual of theirs, the honest and true part. Begun by Zach when Lou asked him outright if he sincerely loved her with his whole heart.

"Won't it be terrific, just the two of us alone?"

"Yes, it will."

Louisa wasn't worried about what her mother would have described as her "womanly virtue." They had already decided not to go that far until after they were wed, and she trusted Zach to keep his word. Trusted him as much as she trusted herself. Which was ironic, considering that at the time of her father's death the only person she trusted was her pa.

After another few yards Zach reined up, rising in the saddle to cock his head. "Did you hear that?"

"Hear what?" The only sound Louisa heard was the gentle rustling of aspen leaves.

"It sounded like a scream."

"No."

Zach listened for a minute, positive his ears hadn't deceived him. He took pride in the keenness of his hearing and his other senses. From childhood he had honed them to be the best they could be, so that one day he would be worthy of being the great warrior he'd always longed to become. But after a minute, when the sound wasn't repeated, he shrugged and sat. "Maybe it was that eagle."

They rode on, Lou forced to fall behind him because the aspens were packed too close together. She hoped he was wrong about the scream. Unfriendly tribes like the Blackfeet, Piegans, and Bloods sent war parties into that area from time to time. Should she fall into their hands, they would force her to be the wife of one of their warriors. Stalking Coyote would be viciously tortured.

Just then a piercing cry wavered on the wind. This time there was no mistaking it for a bird of prey.

Zach drew reins and lifted his Hawken.

"Goodness gracious!" Lou breathed. It had been horrible, the screech of a soul in mortal agony. And it came from just over the ridge. "Let's get out of here."

"We can't." Zach listened a bit, then kneed the dun forward. "Stay close and keep your eyes skinned. If it's a war party, they may have lookouts."

Louisa couldn't believe him sometimes. "What in

26

tarnation are you doing? It's none of our business. We should leave while we still can!''

Zach didn't take his eyes off the crest. ''Someone's in trouble. And my pa always helps folks in need.''

Her pa had always done the same, but Lou would still rather apply her heels and ride hell-bent for leather. ''It might be a white man,'' she mentioned, fully aware Zach wasn't very fond of whites thanks to the years of abuse he had suffered for being a ''half-breed.''

''It might,'' Zach acknowledged, and surprised himself by climbing higher. He really didn't share his father's fondness for lending a helping hand. Or he didn't *think* he did. So what was he trying to prove? He should whisk Louisa out of there. But curiosity, or something else, compelled him to keep going.

''Men!'' Lou fumed, and was dismayed by her remark. Not because she was upset at Zach, the one she cared for more than any other, but because she sounded just like her mother. Countless times she had heard her mother say the very same thing. And as much as Lou had loved her ma, she'd vowed never to turn out like her. Could it be she would, after all? Had her grandmother been right when she said all little girls grow up to become their mothers?

Another scream rent the wilds, spooking sparrows into flight. Whoever it was suffered horribly.

Louisa grasped her rifle tighter, the hairs at the nape of her neck prickling. She'd heard stories about the atrocities Indians sometimes committed, about bodies terribly mutilated, about fingers and toes hacked off, tongues ripped out, eyes gouged from their sockets. In her mind's eye she saw a hapless mountain man being tormented by leering Bloods or Piegans. So she was all the more bewildered when they reached the top, slid off their horses, and peered down into the next valley. From their vantage point they could see into a clearing in a belt of dense woodland.

''They're all white men!'' Louisa blurted.

27

"So they are," Zach said. Eight, all told, one apparently asleep, a younger man at his side. Across the clearing, an oldster had been tied to a trunk. Dwarfing him was a hulking brute almost the size of Zach's father. The brute wielded a long knife. Four others watched intently.

Lou saw the blade flash. "Why, they're whittling on that old-timer! Why would they do a thing like that?"

Zach had no idea. Another scream greeted the slash. Zach was sure he saw a red rivulet flow from the wound, even at that distance. "I know him."

"Who?"

"That old one." Zach had to think a bit before he recollected the details. "Saw him at the rendezvous a few times. His name is Frazier. He's a friend of Shakespeare McNair's." Who, in turn, was mentor to Zach's father. "He also stopped at our cabin once, about eight years ago. Pa and him played checkers half the night."

"Then let's go fetch your pa," Lou suggested. "He'll know what to do." She said it mainly to keep Zach from getting involved. Ruffians who would cut up an old man like Frazier would have no qualms about doing the same, or worse, to a "half-breed."

"It would take too long." Zach eased onto his belly and snaked to a flat boulder. Slowly rising, he studied the lower portion of the ridge. There was no cover to speak of. Until they were below tree level, they would be exposed, easy for the men in the clearing to spot. "We'll have to swing around to the south."

"You're going to help this man you hardly know?"

"Need you ask?"

"But he's white," Lou reiterated in a bid to convince Stalking Coyote to change his mind. She couldn't bear to see him hurt. Not ever.

Zach was no fool. Her motive was as plain as the dainty nose on her pretty face. "Frazier never treated me as most do. He never had that look in his eyes when we met."

28

"What look?"

"That gleam they get, the ones who hate 'breeds. The ones who have to choke back their hatred just to be civil. The ones who think people like me should be squashed like bugs." Zach's jaw muscles twitched. "The ones who have no right to go on breathing."

The tone he used held a world of meaning. Lou accepted she would not be able to convince him, and said, "All right. How do we go about saving the old codger?"

"We?"

"What you do, I do."

Zach had another of his many daily urges to kiss her. "It's too dangerous. You'll stay with the horses and come on the fly when I give a holler."

"Like hell I will."

Rarely did Lou swear. Zach looked at her, impressed by her determination but just as determined to keep her safe. "Only one of us can sneak—" he began, but she wouldn't let him finish.

"Let's get something straight here and now. I'm not one of those gals who will sit around twiddling her thumbs while her man goes off to risk life and limb. I meant it when I said that what you do, I do. I refuse to be like my ma, no matter what my grandma believed."

"What do they have to do with it?"

"My ma always stayed at home while pa went off to work. She never had a job of her own, never had anything to do except housework. She sewed and cleaned and scrubbed until her hands were blistered, all because she loved us and wanted us to have a clean house and nice clothes. But she never got to go out and *do* anything. She never got to really *live*. I won't do the same. I refuse to spend my life chained to a washcloth."

"I still don't see—" Zach tried to get in a word edgewise, but Lou raised a hand to silence him.

"You've asked me to be your wife. You want us to

be a couple. Then we have to live as a couple should. The things you like to do, I'll do, too. Things I like, you should take the time to share. That's how two people who are in love should be.''

Lou paused, and Zach waited. He didn't have the foggiest notion what this had to do with rescuing Frazier, but he decided it was best to let her vent her spleen so he could get on with what needed to be done.

"When there's danger, we'll face it together. I'm not about to cower in a corner while you go off to slay dragons.''

Zach couldn't help himself. "Dragons?'' She was being ridiculous, but he refrained from saying so. What was it Shakespeare McNair once said? "Zach, my boy, the important thing to remember about women is that they're *always* right. Even when they're wrong, they're right. It's a basic law of nature, and the sooner you accept it, the better off you'll be.''

"You know what I mean,'' Lou said, clasping his hand. "Please, Stalking Coyote. Don't be like my pa. As much as I loved him, I'd never marry someone like him.''

Gruff laughter from below spurred Zach into motion. They could hash over the "couple" business later. Those men in the valley might take it into their heads to make wolf meat of poor Frazier at any moment. "Come with me.''

Louisa was elated. He had understood her exactly, just as she had always foreseen the love of her life would do. Stalking Coyote wasn't like most men. He listened to her, took her feelings into account, and was wise enough to give in when he was wrong. Their marriage would be nothing like the union of her ma and pa. They would get along perfectly, never spatting, never squabbling over trifles. It was all she could do not to throw her arms around him and hold him close.

When they were clear of the rim, Zach rose and hastened to the horses. Every minute counted. Swinging up, he trotted to the south, skirting the ridge and entering the valley. Trees screened them until they reached a strip of high grass. "You wait here."

"I'll do no such thing," Louisa asserted. "Didn't you hear a word I said back there? Don't tell me you're one of those men who let everything a woman says go in one ear and out the other."

Sliding off, Zach shoved his Hawken at her. "Take this and wait."

"You didn't listen!" Louisa said, appalled. How could she have misjudged him so badly?

"When you hear a shot, come in hard and fast. I'm counting on you to get there quick. If you don't, I won't live long enough to be your husband." So saying, Zach crouched and glided into the grass.

He was counting on her! The words pealed in Louisa's mind like bells in a church, and she grinned in triumph. He had been paying attention! And he was proving the depth of his devotion by putting his life in her hands! *Oh, how she adored him!*

Zachary King made a beeline for the clearing. He was through the grass and in among the pines when yet another wail rang out. Drawing a flintlock, he advanced on cat's feet, dropping flat when movement ahead hinted he was near enough to be seen.

Zach was glad Lou hadn't raised a fuss about being left behind. He simply couldn't put her in peril. Being a couple was well and good, but that didn't mean they wore each other's pants. He was the warrior, not she. He had counted coup, he had held his own against Sioux and Apaches. So he was the one who should rightfully confront these strangers.

Voices grew in volume.

From behind a log, Zach watched as the big man with the knife waved it under Frazier's nose. "How much longer do you think you can hold out, old man? Why not make it easy on yourself and tell us what we want?"

31

The gray-haired trapper raised his head, his mouth moving as if he were trying to spit in the big man's face. Either his mouth was too dry or he was too weak, because he sagged and said weakly, "Do your worst, bastard. I'd rather die."

A small man with an uncanny resemblance to a rat gripped Frazier's beard. "You've got grit, mister. We'll grant you that. But you're also as stupid as the day is long. Vince Kendrick is a wizard at carving people down to size. He can go on sticking that steel into you until you beg him to stop. Trust me. I've seen him do it before."

Fury lent Frazier the energy to rasp, "I wouldn't trust you as far as I can throw a bull buffalo! Kill me and be done with it!"

"Not on your life," Kendrick said, and chuckled as if he had made a joke. Elbowing the ratlike man away, he held the dripping knife close to the trapper's left eye. "What will it be next? Maybe this eyeball? Or how about if I cut off your nose? Or an ear?"

Incredibly, Frazier arced a knee at the bigger man's groin. But Kendrick skipped backward, bumping into one of the others. Another tittered, earning a glare. Kendrick then stalked to their captive and seized Frazier by the shirt. "That's how you want to be? Fine. Forget your eye or your nose. What I'm fixing to cut off is a lot lower down." To demonstrate, he dipped the blade below his waist.

Zach had witnessed enough. He couldn't let the torture go on. Crawling to the left to come up on the tree from the rear, he stopped when the young man who had been on the other side of the clearing joined the rest.

"Mr. Kendrick, that tea the old man made is doing wonders. Frank's quieted down and is sleeping like a baby."

"That's nice, Billy," Kendrick said without turning. "Go back and stay with him while we show our guest how grateful we are."

Billy pivoted but didn't obey. Visibly mustering courage, he said, "It ain't right, Mr. Kendrick."

"What isn't?"

"To treat Mr. Frazier like you're doing. He never did anything to deserve it. I wish you'd let him go."

"Do as you were told, boy."

"Please, Mr. Kendrick. As a favor to me."

The big man, hissing like an agitated serpent, spun. From a pocket he produced a pouch and shook it. "Are you blind? Didn't you see what was in here?"

"Sure, I saw. And it's not ours. Taking it would be stealing."

Amazement etched Vince Kendrick's face. "Are you addlepated? After all the trouble we went to, all the suffering, and you want us to go on home flat broke?"

"It's not ours," Billy repeated. "What we're doing is wrong."

"Boy, you have a lot to learn. Being right or wrong depends on which end of the gun or knife you are. We can be rich, Billy. *Rich.* We can have more money than we ever would have earned raising plews. Think of it! Everything you've ever wanted, yours for the taking. And the only thing standing in our way is this stubborn jackass."

Zach resumed circling. If he could get the drop on them, he'd free Frazier and guide the old-timer to the grass. Once on the dun, he would use all the tricks he'd learned from his father and his Shoshone friends to elude the cutthroats.

"I'm tired of you pestering me," Kendrick was saying. "So if you want equal shares for your brother and you, scat. Or the rest of us will divide it up five ways."

Five! Kendrick had said five! Zach remembered seeing that many near the old trapper earlier, but now there were only four, plus Billy. One of them had disappeared while Lou and he were riding down the ridge. But where to?

The answer came in the form of a distinct metallic click as a gun muzzle was jammed against his temple.

Chapter Three

"One wrong move and I'll splatter your brains from here to kingdom come."

The barrel was pulled back a few inches, allowing Zach King to turn his head. A lean broomstick in a brown homespun shirt and pants with holes at the knees was eyeing him as if he were a mountain lion about to spring.

"Do you savvy the white man's tongue, you red devil?"

Zach realized the broomstick mistook him for an Indian. Which was easy to do, given how he was dressed and the style in which he wore his hair. His green eyes would give the truth away, but the broomstick hadn't noticed. Should he reveal who he was? In light of how they were treating Frazier, he didn't think it would make much difference. "Yes, I understand English," he answered.

The broomstick blinked. "You do? Will wonders never cease." His finger was wrapped around the trigger, his thumb twitching on the hammer. "Let go of your flintlock and sit up. Do it real slow.''

Zach did as he was told. The man had him discard his other pistol and his knife, then raise his hands over his head and stand.

"Start walking toward camp. I'll have you covered the whole way, so don't try anything. Nothing would give me greater pleasure than to blow a window in your skull."

Yet another Indian-hater. Zach wanted to beat his own head against a boulder for letting himself be taken by surprise. He had been unforgivably careless. Shoshone warriors like Touch the Clouds and Drags the Rope would never be caught with their guard down. It shamed him.

The group in the clearing saw Zach being escorted in and stopped arguing. Several raised rifles and fanned out. All were glancing every which way, as if in fear of being attacked, and the big one, Vince Kendrick, exclaimed, "An Indian! Here! Where the hell did you find him, Sanders?"

"Spying on us over yonder," the broomstick said, then bragged, "I snuck right up on him without him noticing."

The rat-faced man was greatly agitated. "I don't like this, boys. I don't like this one bit. Where there's one stinking Injun, there are always more. There could be a whole war party out there, waiting to pounce."

"Calm down, Stark," Kendrick said. "They won't dare jump us while we have one of their own."

A pudgy man in a floppy hat was more scared than anyone. "I say we light a shuck. My grandpa was killed by heathens. Butchered, he was. I was only ten and puked my guts out when I saw it."

Kendrick did not like having his authority challenged. "I'm the one who says what we'll do and what we won't. Rein in your nerves, Cyrus. I want you to take Johnson"—he pointed at a short man who had the build of a blacksmith—"and go have a look-see. Make a sweep of the woods, then report back."

The pudgy man looked at the shadowy forest and blanched. "You want us to go in there? Forget it, Vince. I'll be damned if I will."

"You'll be damned if you don't," Kendrick said, pointing his pistol. "You've been with me long enough to know I never bluff. Either you go check like I want, or so help me, I'll shoot you where you stand."

Scowling fiercely, Cyrus tromped off with Johnson in tow. The vegetation closed around them.

"I swear," Vince Kendrick griped. "The next son of a bitch who sasses me is going to have his skull split."

Zach saw that Frazier was unconscious. The old man's stomach and chest bore half a dozen knife wounds, all bleeding profusely. But they weren't as severe as they seemed. Kendrick had not cut deep and had avoided vital organs. Zach braced himself when the big man suddenly swiveled toward him.

"Anyone have any idea what tribe this redskin is from?"

No one did. The broomstick shook his head, saying, "I should have asked. He speaks our lingo, Vince. Speaks it real good, too."

"Is that a fact?"

Kendrick studied Zach closely. Zach tucked his chin so the man couldn't see his eyes. He considered making a break for it. Only four men ringed him, and only two had him covered.

"What tribe do you belong to, Indian?"

"I am an Ute," Zach lied. Maybe a bluff could succeed where he had failed. "And I am not alone. Twenty warriors are nearby. Harm me, and they will hunt you down and slay you all."

"Oh, Lord!" Billy declared. "Utes are some of the worst! Remember what that feller we met a while back said? They kill every white man they catch in their territory."

Ed Stark was staring at the trees as if a horde of

savages were about to pour out. "Let's get the hell out of here while we still can!"

Without any warning, Vince Kendrick stepped over to Stark and backhanded him across the cheek. The force of the blow knocked Stark to his knees. Kendrick hiked his pistol, on the verge of bashing in the other's noggin. But, quivering with suppressed rage, Kendrick slowly lowered his arm. "We'll leave when I say, not before."

Zach had come to a couple of conclusions. First, Kendrick wasn't very bright, but he had a mean streak as wide as the Divide. The man ran roughshod over the others, and some of them resented it. This was useful knowledge Zach might be able to use to his advantage. Second, these men were greeners, relatively new to the mountains. True mountaineers would have sought cover the instant they knew Indians were in the vicinity.

Kendrick pivoted. "Now, as for you, Indian," he poked his pistol against Zach's ribs, "if those friends of yours give us a lick of grief, you'll be the first to die. I guarantee it."

"Let me go and we will let you leave in peace," Zach said.

Snorting, Kendrick responded, "Just like that? Do you reckon we fell out of the clouds during the last rainstorm? If we set you free, what's to stop your friends from turning us into pincushions?"

"You have my word."

Kendrick and Sanders laughed. Billy was too busy wringing his hands and glancing at his brother to share their humor. As for Ed Stark, he was slowly rising, rubbing his cheek and smoldering with indignation at how he had been treated.

"Take the word of a lousy savage?" Kendrick said. "That's the craziest thing I've ever heard." Sobering, he gouged the barrel deeper into Zach. "No, I have a better idea. What's your name?"

"Stalking Coyote."

"I hope those warriors out there are good pards of yours, Stalking Coyote, because if just one of my men takes an arrow, you pay the price. You're our insurance. So long as we have you, no one will lift a finger against us."

The man's logic was flawed. Were there really Utes in the woods, they would pick the whites off in a volley of lead and arrows that would drop the fools where they stood. "Will you release me later?" he asked, secretly girding himself to make a bid for freedom.

"Sure we will," Kendrick said. "On that you have *my* word."

The big man's pledge, Zach reflected, was as worthless as teats on a bull buffalo. The brute intended to slay him once the whites felt they were safe—no doubt after doing to him as they had done to Frazier.

No sooner did the thought cross Zach's mind than the old trapper groaned and stirred. Frazier's eyelids fluttered and he looked up. "Never tell you," he mumbled. "Not in a million years." He gazed straight at Zach, and for a few seconds Zach feared Frazier would recognize him and blurt something that would give the cutthroats a clue to who he really was. But the trapper merely groaned once again and lapsed into unconsciousness.

Zach exhaled in relief. But it was short-lived. For a moment later, Vince Kendrick hauled off and punched him in the stomach.

Louisa May Clark was beside herself. It was taking Stalking Coyote much longer than she thought it should. She anxiously scanned the tree line for sign of him, but the minutes continued to drag by and he never appeared.

Tempted to go after him, Lou nervously gnawed on her lower lip. Should she or shouldn't she? Zach had specifically told her to wait, and he might be mad if she didn't. But what if he was in trouble? She was the only one who could help.

Climbing down, Lou paced at the edge of the grass. She had a feeling something was wrong, and the feeling grew as more time went by. At last she couldn't take the suspense. After tying both sets of reins to a small fir, she jogged off, a rifle in each hand.

Once in the woods, the quiet unnerved her. Birds should be chirping, chipmunks chattering. But it was as still as a graveyard at midnight.

Inadvertently, Lou stepped on a dry twig that snapped. Freezing, she waited with bated breath for an outcry or a shot. Her confidence boosted when nothing happened, she moved toward the clearing.

Lou had not gone another dozen feet when she detected movement off to the left. Squatting, she set down Zach's Hawken and pressed her own to her shoulder. She hoped it was he, but then tall bushes parted and two figures materialized. They were two of the men who had been in the clearing, a pudgy fellow and another built like an anvil. Back to back, rifles level, they prowled closer, evidently searching for someone.

For her? Lou regretted being so rash; she should have done as Stalking Coyote wanted. She fixed a bead on the pudgy one, who was facing her. From his expression he seemed to be scared to death, although what he had to be scared of was a mystery. Then the pudgy one whispered to the other loud enough for her to overhear.

"I say we've looked long enough, Johnson. Let's go back."

The anvil lowered his rifle a trifle. "We can't, Cyrus. We haven't made a complete sweep of the area, like Kendrick wanted."

"To hell with Mr.-High-and-Mighty. There hasn't been any sign of any more savages."

"That doesn't mean a thing," Johnson said. "They're like ghosts. For all we know, the whole war party is watching us right this minute."

"All the more reason for us to head back. Or do

you want to lose your scalp?'' Cyrus sidled to his left. ''I don't much like the notion of throwing my life away. I have a wife and two sprouts back home, and I aim to see them again someday.''

Johnson hesitated, gave the forest a final scrutiny, then trailed the pudgy man off into the pines.

Louisa was more confused than ever. What was that about savages? And a war party? If it was true, she must warn Zach. Hefting his Hawken, she let the two men get a good lead, then shadowed them. When the clearing came into sight she veered to the right. Men were moving about. Horses nickered. A broad pine offered a convenient haven from which to observe the goings-on.

Cyrus and Johnson were just walking into the open. Others were saddling mounts, wrapping blankets, extinguishing the fire. A young man, not much older than Zach, was helping someone who appeared to be sick, stand. Frazier was still tied to the trunk.

Lou did not see her beloved until a big man near the trapper moved. Icy terror lanced through her at the sight of Stalking Coyote on his knees, his arms over his stomach. In her fear for his welfare she almost leaped from concealment to rush to his side.

''Anything?'' the big man asked Johnson and Cyrus.

''Not a trace,'' the pudgy one said.

''But they're out there, Kendrick,'' Johnson quickly mentioned. ''I swear I could feel their eyes on me at one point.'' He surveyed the woodland. ''I have the same feeling now.''

Kendrick scowled and put his hands on his hips. ''Just so they keep their distance. Saddle up, boys. We're leaving.''

''Where to?'' Cyrus asked.

''You'll see soon enough. I have an idea how to find out exactly how many Indians we're up against. And maybe cut the odds. So hustle. We only have four hours of daylight left, and it will take us half that to reach the spot I have in mind.''

Louisa, aghast, saw them bind Zach's wrists behind his back. A packhorse was brought and he was roughly thrown over it, facedown. The sick man had to be boosted onto his mount, and he was so weak, he nearly fell off. So the young one climbed up behind him. Soon they were ready to leave. Frazier had been tied on a mule, and blood trickled down his saddle as Kendrick led the whole bunch to the northwest.

Ducking from view, Lou stayed where she was until the hoofbeats faded. Then she uncoiled and ran as she had never run before. At any second she expected hostiles to burst out of nowhere, but none did, and within five minutes she was on the mare and trotting in pursuit of those who dared endanger her betrothed.

It consoled her, somewhat, that Stalking Coyote had not been gravely hurt. Her main concern was how long he would *stay* that way. Kendrick might take it into his head to kill Zach at any time. Somehow, she must save him. And the old trapper, if at all possible.

Squaring her slender shoulders, Louisa May Clark rode deeper into the dark heart of the merciless wilderness.

A man could learn a lot if he kept his mouth shut and his ears open.

Zach King did not say two words over the next two hours, but he heard a lot, comments that painted a telling portrait of the members of the band. Ed Stark and Ira Sanders, for instance, had been with Kendrick longer than the rest. Billy and Frank Batson were simple farmers who had let dreams of wealth lead them astray. Cyrus Walton had been a clerk who tired of scribbling in ledgers all day and decided to take part in the grand adventure of trapping beaver. That left Elden Johnson, the quiet one of the bunch, who never said enough to give Zach a clue to what he had done before he joined the ill-fated ''brigade.''

It was Johnson who brought up the rear and was always shifting in the saddle to scour the countryside. About three hours after they left the clearing, Johnson galloped to the head of the line and consulted briefly with Kendrick. As he was returning, Johnson slowed to sneer at Zach and say, "They're back there, sure enough. I just caught sight of a couple of them off in the trees. But don't get your hopes up, vermin. Vince has a surprise in store for them." Cackling, he went on.

Zach knew better. No Indians were back there. It had to be Lou, following them. She was being lured right into whatever trap Kendrick had cooked up.

Cyrus Walton held the lead rope to the packhorse. Glancing over a heavyset shoulder, he remarked, "Pretty soon all your friends will be so much buzzard bait."

"You are wrong, white man," Zach said, pretending to be confident when in truth worry ate at him like acid. "Harm one of my people and the whole tribe will be after you. Can you fight off two thousand warriors?"

Cyrus's thick mouth puckered. "Two thousand, my ass! Maybe I haven't fought many redskins, but I know there's never that many in a single village."

"One village, no. Five villages, yes."

"Five?"

Zach laid it on as thick as pine sap. "In the summer all my people gather at a river south of here. We feast, dance, meet old friends. Every Ute warrior in the Ute nation is present."

"Maybe I should have a talk with Vince." Cyrus rubbed his double chin. "For an Indian, you sure do speak English good. Where'd you learn?"

"From a missionary," Zach fibbed.

"You mean to say the Utes would give a Bible-thumper the time of day?" The former clerk rose in the saddle to see beyond the packhorse. "Two thousand? Damn. We wouldn't stand a prayer."

Zach twisted his head to verify that no one else was within earshot. "Let me go, Walton. I will tell my people you are my friend and they will spare you."

"You're just trying to trick me," Cyrus said.

"Suit yourself. But what do you have to lose? Do nothing, and you will be killed with the others when my people catch up."

"I don't know."

Inwardly smiling, Zach said, "Even if your friends lay an ambush, it is unlikely they will kill all the warriors who follow us. A messenger will be sent to the gathering, and all of you will be wiped out."

It had an effect. Cyrus Walton became a bundle of apprehension. His eyes darted back and forth and he licked his lips again and again. A quarter of an hour elapsed. Then Cyrus slowed so his bay was alongside the packhorse. Softly, he said, "You mean it, Indian? About sparing me if I help you?"

"When an Ute makes a promise, he keeps it," Zach said. That happened to be true. The Utes were honorable in all their dealings.

"I still don't know," Cyrus said.

But Zach did. He had the man hooked. Walton wanted to live more than anything. Manipulating him would be simple. "Think on it. But do not think too long. In less than an hour we will be wherever Kendrick is taking us, and I must stop him from killing any of my people."

The fish didn't take the bait. "Even if I wanted to, I couldn't do anything until well after dark, when everyone will be asleep."

That would be much too late. Zach racked his brain for a way of persuading Walton, but he was denied the opportunity. Cyrus suddenly went as rigid as a board and said, "Kendrick is watching us! I can't make him suspicious." Slapping his legs against the bay, he pulled ahead as far as the lead rope allowed.

Frustration coursed through Zach. Lou was going to

ride right into their clutches, and he was helpless to help her.

The thud of hooves heralded Vince Kendrick, who wheeled his horse so it walked beside the pack animal. "What were Walton and you just jabbering about?" he demanded bluntly.

"He wanted to know why my people hate whites so much."

"Why do they?"

"Whites kill our game. They take beaver from our streams. They come and go as they please, as if the land our forefathers have lived in for countless winters is theirs." Zach had heard enough complaints from various tribes to rattle off a list as long as his arm. But Kendrick wasn't really interested.

"That's all you talked about?"

"Yes."

"Nothing else?"

"If you do not believe me, ask him."

Kendrick dismissed the idea with a curt oath. "What good would that do? He'd only lie through his teeth to spare his hide. But just so you'll know, I have a hunch what you're up to, and I'll be keeping my eyes on you." A flick of his reins and he was gone.

Kendrick had spoken loud enough for Walton to hear, deliberately, to put a scare into him. And from the fearful glance Walton gave the big man as he rode by, it had worked.

Zach fought down a wave of despair. He was on his own. He must escape and reach Lou, and he must do it quickly. Time was running out.

A series of rolling, wooded hills had brought them to a broad meadow over half a mile long. Vince Kendrick hollered and pointed at the far end where a bluff reared skyward. It was the key to the trap, Zach guessed. From up there, the whites could see for miles in all directions. No one could approach unseen. They would lie up there and wait for the Utes to show.

But it was sweet Louisa who would be in their gun sights.

Desperate, Zach glanced back at the trees. They were sixty feet away. Only one rider, Elden Johnson, was between him and Lou's salvation. All Zach had to do was get past Johnson and he could give the whites the slip.

Precious seconds were wasting.

Zach flung himself backward and rolled when he hit, rolling over and over until he was well into the high grass. Someone—Johnson, was it?—yelled to alert the others. Coming to rest on his back, Zach tucked his knees to his chest and levered his wrists down over his buttocks and his moccasins so his hands were in front of him. Then, pumping upward, he sprinted madly toward the pines.

"Stop him!" Vince Kendrick roared.

A shot blasted. Lead sizzled the air close to Zach's ear.

"Not like that, you idiot!" Kendrick bellowed. "We need him alive, remember?"

Zach ran flat out. The grass clung to his legs like vines, but he didn't let it slow him down; the whites were converging on him like a pack of rabid wolves. Foremost was Elden Johnson. Out of the corner of an eye Zach saw Johnson narrow the gap and elevate his rifle as if it were a club. Leaning outward, Johnson grinned in sadistic anticipation.

Zach had to time it just right. He waited until the very last instant, until Johnson was on top of him and the rifle stock swept at his head. Then Zach vaulted to the right, recovered his balance, and sprang, grabbing at Johnson's waist as the white man galloped by.

Fate served Zach cruelly. Had he been as large and as strong as his father, he could have thrown Johnson to the ground. But Johnson was too bulky, too powerful, and although Zach strained and pulled, Johnson stayed in the saddle.

To go on trying would be useless. Zach dropped,

stumbled a few feet, and took off for the trees like an antelope fleeing a fire. Forty feet! That was all he had to cover! But it might as well be forty miles, because no man alive could outrun a horse and Johnson had already reined around to intercept him.

"Stop the son of a bitch!" Kendrick raged.

Thirty-five feet. Thirty. Zach darted to the left, hooves thundering at his heels. Again the stock of Johnson's rifle narrowly missed him. Again Zach lunged, but at the Kentucky, not at Johnson. Wrapping his hands around the barrel, he wrenched, seeking to unhorse his adversary. Instead, he ripped the rifle from the man's grasp.

Johnson, hauling on the mount's reins, clawed for a pistol.

A bound brought Zach close enough. The stock caught Johnson on the ear, crushing cartilage and toppling him like a felled oak.

An empty saddle beckoned. Zach leaped, but the spooked horse bolted. Zach's fingers closed on empty air. Thwarted, he dashed toward the woods, the hammering of heavy hooves rising in a crescendo. Ed Stark and Ira Sanders were almost on top of him. Twisting, Zach trained the Kentucky on them and both swerved wide.

Kendrick, farther back, was livid. *"What the hell are you doing? Don't let him reach the trees! Shoot him if you have to!"*

"But you said not to!" Stark responded.

"Do what I tell you!"

Stark and Sanders raised their rifles. Zach immediately started zigzagging. Another eighteen feet and he would be there! A gun cracked, the ball thudding into the soil rather than his flesh. He cut to the left, to the right.

"He's worse than a rabbit!" Ed Stark complained.

Zach covered the last four yards and streaked between a pair of saplings. He'd done it! About to angle toward a thicket, he couldn't resist a last glance, couldn't resist flashing a grin at his tormentors. And when he did, he saw Vince Kendrick, who had stopped to take steady aim. He saw Kendrick at the exact split second that Kendrick's rifle spewed smoke. Then a ten-ton tree fell on him—or so it felt like—and he pitched into an inky well, falling down, down, down into oblivion.

Chapter Four

Louisa May Clark had lost sight of the cutthroats. She'd been staying well back so they wouldn't spot her, but when long minutes passed and she didn't see so much as a flicker of movement ahead, she worried that she had fallen too far behind and brought the mare to a gallop. So intent was she on catching up that she failed to realize she was approaching a meadow until the blast of a rifle brought her to a halt and she spied grass off through the trees.

Panicked, thinking they had seen her and that she was their target, Lou reined the mare around and led Zach's dun into dense growth. When more shots boomed and none of the slugs came anywhere near her, Lou deduced that Kendrick and company were shooting at someone else. Indians, she thought. But no war whoops punctuated the din. She wondered if maybe they were fighting among themselves. Then a third possibility dawned on her, and she came close to flying out into the meadow to find out.

It might be Zach they were trying to kill! The

thought chilled her like a wintry icy rain. Love and caution waged a bitter struggle in her heart and caution won, but by a whisker. A commotion erupted near the end of the trees. Intervening vegetation prevented her from seeing who was involved, but at length the vague forms retreated. After waiting what she judged to be a suitable interval, Lou moved forward.

The men were well out on the meadow. Lou saw her precious Zach, draped over the same packhorse. She couldn't be sure, but she thought his legs as well as arms were bound now. Kendrick was at the rear of the line, talking to the man called Johnson, who had a strip of cloth wrapped around his head.

Confusion plagued Lou. If the cutthroats hadn't been firing at Zach, what was all that shooting about? Indians were the logical bet, but none was anywhere to be seen.

Lou did see a high bluff, though, and that posed a problem. Clearly, Kendrick's men were making straight for it. Any simpleton could figure out why. They'd spot her if she tried to cross the meadow, so either she must take the long way around or she should wait until dark. Against her every instinct, she dismounted.

To say the next few hours passed at a snail's pace would be an understatement. For Lou, every second was an eternity of unendurable suspense and awful fear. Not fear for herself, but for the one who had claimed her heart.

She used to believe that she was immune to the fickle barbs of outrageous Cupid, that she would go through her whole life without ever growing attached to any man. That the tapestry of her life was meant to unravel alone. Always alone. *How could any man ever care for me?* she'd often asked herself. *What would a male ever see in me?* She was so plain, so ordinary, she never merited a second glance from the boys she passed on the street.

Her mother once told her such feelings were normal.

That practically every girl went through a bout of doubt. Many could never accept they were attractive enough, or charming enough, to earn the attention of the opposite sex. "But the truth, child, is that everyone has a true love somewhere. Think of it as two people being two halves of the same coin. And when those halves are joined, no force in Creation can rend them asunder." Lou's mother had stroked her hair. "Don't fret. Sooner or later you'll meet the handsome prince you're destined to meet. And from that day on, he will be the only one for you."

Lou had asked, "Is Pa the other half of your coin, then?"

"Yes, he is," Mary Bonham Clark said without hesitation. "Oh, I know we squabble now and then. I know he sorely tries my soul with his wild schemes. But in spite of his shortcomings, he's the man I was meant to marry. I wouldn't trade him for anyone."

Her mother's devotion, even when times were bleak, had impressed Lou immensely. " 'For better or worse' is how the vow goes. What kind of woman would I be if I only stood by Zebulon when things are going smoothly?"

It was her mother's loyalty, more than anything else, that convinced Lou maybe men weren't as bad as some women claimed. Her aunt Edna, for instance, had always gone on and on about how men were children in oversize bodies. "Look at how they act! They always have to do things *their* way, and when they can't, they sulk like five-year-olds. And talk about tempers! Try to give a man advice and he treats you as if you bashed him with a rock. Why the Almighty ever made us depend on them to perpetuate the human race, I'll never know. Were it up to me, I'd just as soon buy babies from a general store."

Aunt Edna always did say the strangest things.

Lou's meandering thoughts returned to the present. The cutthroats were at the bluff, winding up a trail on the north side. Soon they would be on the crest. In another hour the sun would set, and then Lou would venture into the open. She could hardly wait. To while away the time, she checked both rifles and her flint-locks, confirming all were loaded.

Something told her that before the night was done, she would have need of them.

Zach King was at the bottom of a bottomless well, immersed in pitch-black gloom, blackness so complete it withered the soul. It was as if the universe had blinked out and he were the only living creature left. Nothingness sheathed him like a sheath would a knife. He flailed his arms, or thought he did, and felt black-ness swish through his fingers. It was so real, this ethe-real blackness, as if endowed with form and substance.

Gradually his mind filtered the memory of being shot. Zach dreaded that the blackness was the sum total of the afterlife. Maybe both the Heaven of the whites and the Land of Coyote, as the Shoshones re-ferred to the hereafter, were fictions. Maybe this was all there was. Maybe he would spend the rest of for-ever there in the depths of the inky domain. The thought made him groan aloud.

"The son of a bitch is coming around, Vince."

The harsh voice shattered the veil like thunder shat-tering benighted heavens. Zach knew he was alive, and with the realization a towering wave of sheer pain crashed down over him, agony so exquisite he had to clench his teeth to keep from crying out so he wouldn't betray weakness in the presence of his ene-mies. Slowly, he opened his eyes.

Beside him hunkered Ed Stark. A dozen feet away sputtered a fire. Around it were hunched Kendrick's followers. The big man himself had risen.

"Damn Injun must have a head as hard as quartz," Stark commented.

Zach begged to differ. His head felt like his mother's mush. Mush being pounded on by a sledge-hammer, for with every beat of his heart another stabbing pang speared through him. He also felt nauseous.

Kendrick's huge frame blotted out stars. "Another inch, heathen, and we'd have left you for the scavengers."

Gingerly, Zach examined his temple. A furrow ran from the hairline to just above his ear. The slug had gouged out flesh and hair nearly down to the skull bone. Dry blood caked the wound, his hair, his ear, his neck. The slightest touch provoked more pain. He wanted to sit up, but his churning stomach rebelled.

"I should shoot you for spoiling my trap," Kendrick said. "Your pards must have heard the shots and hightailed it, because they never showed."

Lou was safe! That alone, Zach reflected, made any sacrifice worth the effort. He swallowed, or tried to, his throat as dry as a desert. "What now, white man?" he asked, still playing the part of a Ute warrior. "Will you let me go?"

"And lose our ace in the hole? Not on your life. So long as we keep you alive, you keep us alive." Kendrick stared into the night. "You'd better hope your friends value your hide more than they value our scalps. Because if they jump us, the boys and I are going to make it a point to turn you into a sieve before we go down."

At that moment, Ira Sanders, who was on the other side of the fire, declared, "This one is coming around too, Vince."

Zach looked over at Ben Frazier. The old trapper was curled on his side, his wrists tied, his bare chest and sides painted scarlet. Sluggishly rising onto his elbows, Frazier crawled toward the fire, probably for the warmth, but Sanders stomped on his forearms, eliciting a yelp of anguish.

"Where do you think you're going?" the scarecrow taunted.

Kendrick walked over and squatted. "You can spare yourself a heap of misery, old man, if you'll tell us where you found it."

Ben Frazier glared at his tormentors. "I'd rather die. So blow out my wick and be done with it, you worthless buzzards."

Zach had to know. "What is it you want of him?" he asked Kendrick. "What can he have that is so important?"

"What do you care?" the big man rejoined.

Ed Stark snapped his fingers, as if struck by inspiration. "Maybe it wouldn't hurt to tell the Injun. His people must know these mountains like the backs of their hands. Could be he's seen some of the g''—Stark caught himself—"some of those pretty yellow stones, and can tell us where."

"Yellow stones?" Zach said.

Kendrick had a pouch. Removing several small objects, he held them out so the firelight played over them. "Take a gander."

Years ago at a rendezvous, a trapper had paraded into the encampment on the Green River bragging about gold he'd found. To prove his claim, he'd brought a handful of nuggets. He never told where he made his strike, but promised to return in a year with enough gold to weigh down a pack train. When he left, several mountaineers sought to trail him, but he shook them off. And that was the last anyone ever saw of him. Some were of the opinion he had been killed and his claim taken over. But there were never any rumors from St. Louis to the effect that someone had shown up with a king's ransom in yellow ore. So others thought a mishap claimed the man's life, taking with it his prized secret.

Zach had seen the fellow's nuggets, and they hadn't much interested him. Being rich was never one of his goals in life. Why should it be, when in the wilderness all the gold in the world amounted to a hill of beans.

"Have you come across any yellow rocks like those?" Ed Stark asked hopefully, his eyes glittering with raw greed.

"No," Zach said.

"Think about it," Stark persisted. "They're usually found along streams and rivers, and your people must have explored every waterway in these parts. Even seen a warrior with the stones like that? Or maybe a squaw? I know how fond Injun women are of pretty trinkets."

"No."

"Damn." Stark sighed and faced Kendrick. "Stupid Injuns. They've probably ridden past the spot a hundred times and were too dumb to know what it was."

The leader replaced the nuggets in the pouch, then regarded the trapper a moment. "Once more, old man. Where did you find it?"

"Are you hard of hearin'?" Frazier replied. "I'll never tell. Do your worst."

"Don't think I won't." And with that, Vince Kendrick kicked Frazier in the ribs. The trapper cried out and tried to wriggle away, but a heavy boot caught him again, lower down. Slowly, methodically, Kendrick delivered one kick after another. Never to the old man's face or neck or anywhere that might kill him. No, Kendrick's intention was to make Frazier suffer, and in that he was ruthlessly effective, for when Kendrick stopped kicking, the trapper was quaking and whimpering.

"Give him a few more," Ira Sanders said.

"Bust a few ribs," Elden Johnson added. "That should loosen his lips."

"It also might kill him," Kendrick said, "and we need the jackass alive." Stooping, he jabbed his fingers into several of the knife wounds. "Enough pain, old man? Or do you want more? I can keep this up all night if need be."

Tears of mixed agony and despair gushed down Frazier's cheeks. His mouth quivered and his hands shook as he feebly clawed at the brute's hands.

Kendrick shook him, as a terrier might shake a rat, or a cat might shake a bird, then flung Frazier onto his back. "Even if you've got all the sand in the world, mister, sooner or later you'll break. One last time. Where?"

Zach half wished the trapper would tell them what they wanted. He admired Frazier's courage, but was the gold worth the cost of Frazier's life? The trapper must think so, because he didn't answer.

"Ed, bring me a brand from the fire."

"Sure thing, Vince."

Zach tested the loops around his wrists and ankles in a futile bid to free himself. He watched as Ed Stark selected a long, thin limb, one end glowing like the red eye of a demon. Stark handed it to Kendrick.

Frazier held himself completely still. Jutting his chin defiantly, he said, "Put out my eyes. Burn me all over. It won't make a difference."

Kendrick blew on the end of the limb, causing the glow to flare brightly. "I'd like to blind you, but you wouldn't be able to see to guide us to the strike. And it would be a waste of time to burn you everywhere when one particular spot will do."

"What spot?" Frazier asked.

Instead of answering, Kendrick growled orders. "Stark, Johnson, hold the old geezer down."

The trapper fought them, but he was too weak to offer stiff resistance. Flat on his back, he glued his gaze to the red tip as it moved in small circles above him.

"Should it be your nose?" Kendrick said, and dipped the brand at Frazier's face. At the last moment, he stopped, chuckling as Frazier cringed and sought to pull away. "Or maybe your neck?" Again Kendrick flicked the brand, but again he didn't press it against the old-timer. "No. I have a better idea." A third time the brand moved, and was poised over Frazier's groin.

"You wouldn't!"

The brand speared downward. A sizzling sound greeted the contact of coal-hot brand and buckskins, and tiny puffs of smoke spiraled starward. Frazier twisted and squirmed, but he was held securely. The sizzling grew louder. Kendrick's visage was a mask of cruel anticipation.

Seconds later Frazier screamed. He couldn't stop himself. No man could. He screamed and bucked as more and more smoke spewed upward.

The smell of burnt buckskin filled Zach's nostrils. Then the pungent odor of burning flesh eclipsed it, and a new scream rent the night, a scream so horrible, so inhuman, it was hard to conceive it issued from Frazier's throat.

Kendrick raised the brand. "That's just a taste, old man. I hardly touched you. Do you want me to go on?"

Zach couldn't fault the trapper for what he did next.

"No, no! Please. Stop! I'll show you!"

"On your honor, old man?" Kendrick puffed on the brand some more. "I wouldn't want you to change your mind come first light. Or to lead us in circles, thinking you might be able to escape later. Because next time I won't stop."

"I promise you. Straight to the gold."

Kendrick tossed the limb into the fire, bent, and patted the trapper's grizzled cheek. "I'm right pleased you've come to your senses. To show there are no hard feelings, I'll have the boys give you some food and water. How'd that be?"

"Fine, just fine," Frazier said, his head slumped, his spirit crushed by his defeat.

"Help him sit up, Ed."

Stark and Johnson boosted the trapper. Frazier, exhausted and emotionally spent, tiredly wiped a sleeve across his face. He looked at the fire, at his tormentors, then to his left. His craggily brow knit. "What's a Shoshone doing here?"

Kendrick walked to Zach, who had turned his face from the light. "Shoshone? All the years you've been in these mountains and you can't you tell one miserable savage from another? This here is an Ute we caught skulking near our camp.''

"But his hair is worn Shoshone-style—'' Frazier began, and suddenly stopped.

Kendrick had jerked Zach off the ground and swung Zach around so the trapper could see Zach's face. "Ever met this buck before? He's mighty educated, for a redskin.''

Zach smiled at the trapper, hoping against hope Frazier would catch on to his ruse and not reveal who he truly was. "Greetings, white man,'' he said. "Any enemy of my enemies is a friend of mine.''

"As I live and breathe! *Zachary King!*''

Louisa waited an hour after the sun went down so it was fully dark when she started across the meadow. As she emerged from the trees, she was perturbed to see the moon rising. Not a quarter moon or a half moon, but a full moon in all its glowing splendor. The lunar lantern would light up the landscape as brightly as twilight. She must hurry. But she couldn't go too fast or the drum of hooves would alert Kendrick's band to her presence.

Holding the mare to a brisk walk, Lou made for the distant bluff. It was too far off to spot even with celestial illumination, but all she had to do was keep pointed due west and she would reach it eventually.

With the advent of night, the wild creatures who preferred darkness to daylight were slinking from their burrows and dens to rove, hunt, and feast. Nighttime was predator time, when the big cats and wolves and grizzlies were most active. So were lesser carnivores, a legion of them. Their howls and yips and roars rose in a bestial chorus that had terrified more than one wayfaring pilgrim from the States.

Lou had grown used to it. Or so she flattered herself. But as she rode farther into the open and the sounds increased in volume and frequency, she grew on edge. It seemed as if a horde of feral beasts were on either side of her, their roars and growls assaulting her ears without cease.

The bleat of a deer so close that it made Lou jump was terminated by a raspy snarl that set the mare to prancing skittishly. Lou had to firm her grip on the reins to keep control. A feline cough pegged the deer's slayer. Thankfully, the mountain lion was content with its catch and didn't molest the horses.

Lou yearned for sight of the bluff. As the minutes dragged by, she worried that she had drifted astray. She debated angling to the right or left. A soft glow over a hundred feet in the air was like a soothing balm on an open sore to her frazzled nerves. Lou relaxed, confident she'd found her quarry. It amused her that Kendrick was dumb enough to make a fire large enough to be seen. *Thank the Lord for stupidity!* Without it, nasty people like Kendrick would cause much more harm than they did.

Lou remembered that the cutthroats had scaled the bluff by using a trail on its north side. She didn't figure the trail would prove difficult to find, but when she reached the base she was confronted by the bane of riders everywhere: a talus slope. A slope so littered with loose rocks and earth that for her to attempt to climb it would result in catastrophe. To say nothing of the racket she would make, a racket bound to be heard by the ruffians above.

Lou rode westward in search of the elusive trail. It had to be there somewhere. She went farther than she thought was necessary and still came across no evidence of it. About to turn around and retrace her steps, she stumbled on a cluster of small boulders.

Just as Lou pulled on the reins, a crisp rattling sound broke out right under the mare's forelegs. Reptilian predators were also abroad at night, and one of them, a rattlesnake, was showing its displeasure at nearly being trod on.

The mare reacted as horses usually did. It snorted and reared, then wheeled and bolted. And there wasn't a thing Lou could do to stop it. She hauled on the reins, but the animal refused to halt. Her right arm stretched to the breaking point, she sought to cling to the reins to Zach's dun. But she also held Zach's Hawken in the same hand, and she couldn't get a solid enough grip on the reins. To her dismay they were wrenched loose, and she was off like a shot, speeding into the vault of darkness on the back of a spooked animal that wouldn't heed her if their lives depended on it.

Which they did.

Into the forest they plunged, low limbs threatening to pluck Lou from her perch or bash in her skull. Branches tore at the mare, adding to its panic. But the greatest danger was from logs and large boulders, deadly obstacles that could cause the mare to tumble.

Lou didn't yell for fear the wind would bear the sound to the top of the bluff. She did say softly, urgently, over and over again, "Stop! Whoa! Slow down! Slow down!"

The mare was too scared.

If Lou had her druthers, she'd let the horse run itself out. But she had to stop it before an accident occurred. She threw her whole weight backward and thrust her feet against the stirrups, but it was like a fly seeking to stop a rabid badger.

Part of the blame lay with the two rifles. Lou couldn't exert her full strength with both hands burdened by Hawkens. She regretted not tying Zach's onto the dun. She regretted it even more when, as the mare sped around a tree, a branch struck her elbow with jarring force, rendering it numb, and Zach's rifle slipped from her grasp.

"No!"

The cry was torn from Lou against her will. She glanced back to see where the Hawken had fallen but couldn't spot it. When she faced front again, she barely had time to duck to avoid the sweep of a limb.

As Louisa straightened, the mare vaulted a log. Another branch loomed out of nowhere, and although Lou tried to sink beneath it, she was struck across the shoulders and ripped from the saddle. Like a child's rag doll, she was thrown to the ground, dashed onto her shoulder, the impact jolting her to her core.

Lou was dimly aware of hoofbeats receding into silence. Well, not quite total silence, for not far off a wolf howled and her own body hammered to the beat of her wildly pumping heart, a hammering as loud as the howl. Lou also realized she had lost her rifle, but finding it had to wait. She needed to take stock of her injuries.

It was a long while, though, before Lou could do anything. Her arm wouldn't move. Her whole side prickled with pain. And deep in her chest it hurt when she breathed. She lay quietly, partly in shock, unwilling to believe the calamity had happened. Gradually, sensation returned to her arm. She moved it in small circles, which lessened some of the pain in her side.

Rolling onto her back, Lou stared up through the canopy of trees at a patch of stars. When she was a little girl she'd liked to makes wishes on stars. She would lie in her bed and gaze out the window, marveling at their number and brightness. They always had a comforting effect, maybe because, when she was three or four, she had asked her grandmother what stars were and her grandma had told her they were angels. For years afterward that was how Lou imagined them, and it soothed her to think the angels were up there watching over her.

They didn't comfort her now. Tonight, the stars seemed to mock her. They were so far away, so elusive, just like Stalking Coyote. Without her help, he would likely die. And she had ruined what might be her best chance to save him.

Grunting, Louisa sat up. Her chest had stopped hurting, which was a good sign, but her arm tingled fiercely, which wasn't. She tried to lift it over her head and nearly cried out from anguish.

The mare was gone. The dun was missing. Zach's rifle might be lost, and hers along with it. She was hurt and alone and stranded afoot in the middle of the wilderness in the dead of night. What else could possibly go wrong?

As if on cue, from the depths of the forest came the ponderous tread of a heavy beast. Thick brush crackled and snapped. Lou groped at her waist and was relieved to find her flintlocks still there.

The thing in the woods uttered a rumbling growl such as only one creature in all the Rockies ever uttered. There could be no doubt what it might be.

The beast stalking toward her was a grizzly.

Chapter Five

Zach King would have dearly loved to have pistols in both hands so he could defend himself, or to be able to race into the night ahead of the hail of lead certain to seek his life now that Vince Kendrick's band knew his secret.

The big man himself was confused. "Zachary King?" he repeated quizzically to Ben Frazier. "What kind of name is that for a Shoshone?"

The old trapper tittered like it was the dumbest question he'd ever heard. "He's not a full-blooded Shoshone, you fool. Any fool could tell just by lookin' at him that he's half white, half Indian. Or didn't you notice his eyes are green?"

"Green?" Swearing, Kendrick dragged Zach closer to the fire and roughly bent Zach's head so the firelight was full on his face. "I'll be damned! They are."

Ed Stark was incensed. "Now that I think about it, he's never looked any of us directly in the eye. All this time he's been playing us for dunces. And laughing at us behind our backs."

"Well, we're going to have the last laugh," Kendrick said. To demonstrate, he drove his fist into their captive's stomach.

Zach doubled over, the breath whooshing from his body. Pinpoints of light swam before his eyes. He was in torment, but he couldn't blame Frazier. The old man had been through hell, had been tortured to the point where he wasn't thinking straight. Otherwise, Frazier would never have blurted the truth. And apparently the old-timer realized his mistake, because as Kendrick cocked a fist, Frazier called out for him to stop.

"Harm that boy and you'll have the whole Shoshone nation down on your heads!"

"I'm not falling for the same trick twice," Kendrick snapped. "This uppity breed claimed he was an Ute, and that *they* would do us in if we harmed so much as a hair on his head." He elevated his fist higher. "I'm going to beat him to death with my bare hands."

Frazier glanced at Zach, his eyes pleading for forgiveness. Then his expression changed to one of seeming indifference. "Go ahead. Kill him if you want. I just pray I live long enough to see his pa turn you into worm food."

Kendrick paused. "His pa?"

"Nate King. Surely you've heard of him? The Indians call him Grizzly Killer. He's as famous as Jim Bridger and Jed Smith."

"King?" Kendrick said. "I've heard that name before."

Ed Stark, always more quick-witted, interjected, "Don't you remember? When we were at Bent's Fort about four months ago? Some of the mountain men were swapping yarns. One brought up this King feller. Said he'd killed more silvertips than anyone. That he's friendly with most of the heathens. And that he's one of the best trackers alive. They say he can track an ant across solid rock."

"Those fools were talking in their cups," Kendrick said. "This 'breed still dies."

Elden Johnson, who rarely had a word to say unless spoken to, had words to say now. "Hold on, Vince. I saw a couple of horses behind us, remember? It could be one man, leading a spare."

"It could be Nate King," Stark clarified, "after his boy."

Kendrick's massive fist slowly lowered, and he shoved Zach to the ground. "Following us, is he? Waiting for the right time to strike? To free you?" Kendrick surveyed the darkness. "He might be out there right this minute, spying on us."

"Probably is," the old trapper agreed. "When it suits him, he'll pick all of you polecats off, one by one. He's not only a fine tracker, but also a crack shot. Won a heap of shootin' contests at the rendezvous. Why, I've seen him put a ball through the center of a coin no bigger than your thumbnail at fifty yards."

It was obvious Kendrick was still inclined to pound Zach to a pulp, but he merely glared and said, "Then I reckon you get to live a while longer yet, 'breed. Your pa won't do anything so long as we can put a bullet into your noggin if he tries."

Stark was deep in thought. "This explains why our ambush didn't work. Nate King is too canny to blunder into our gun sights. To bushwhack him, we need to come up with a better idea."

Pudgy Cyrus Walton was actually relieved. "This sure takes a load of worry off my mind. It's nice to know no savages are going to sneak into camp in the middle of the night and slit our throats. We can get some sleep." He hastily threw in, "Can't we, Vince?"

"I guess we can, at that," Kendrick said. "But I want two men on guard at all times. Frank and Billy will take the first watch."

"Don't forget that food and water you promised me," Ben Frazier said. "I'm so hungry, I could eat a whole buffalo raw."

"We're not about to let you starve, old man," Kendrick responded. "You're too important." He nudged

Zach with a toe. "Which is more than I can say for you, 'breed. As soon as we dispose of your pa, your turn is next. You'll be days dying."

Zach remembered what Kendrick had done to the old trapper, and didn't doubt it.

A grizzly!

Of all the beasts in the mountains, grizzlies were the most formidable. Undisputed lords of their domain, they were as widely feared as they were fearless. They roamed from the highest peaks to the lowland valleys, always in search of food to appease their never-ending hunger. As huge and heavy as buffalo, they were impossibly hard to kill thanks to thick bones and dense sinews. Their teeth could crush a man's thigh in one bite. Claws over four inches long added to their bestial arsenal.

The mere mention of grizzlies had always sparked terror in Louisa. They were more akin to an unstoppable force of Nature than flesh-and-blood animals. Many were the stories she had heard of clashes between trappers and the great bruins, invariably with fatal results for the former. Oh, there was Hugh Glass, mauled so severely by a griz that his companions felt sure he would die, so they abandoned him, just up and walked off to let him greet the Almighty on his own. Only, Glass didn't die. Through sheer willpower he crawled to an Indian village and miraculously recovered. But he was one of few exceptions. By and large, to confront a silvertip was to court death.

Another exception, the most remarkable of all, was Stalking Coyote's pa. Grizzly Killer, he was called, because he had slain more of the great monsters than anyone, ever. Once, Lou had asked him how that could be, and Nate had smiled and said, "Shakespeare McNair likes to say I'm a grizzly magnet. He thinks I draw grizzlies like a magnet draws iron. But I think it had more to do with my being one of the first trappers in the Rockies. Bears were everywhere back then.

Hardly a week went by that I didn't run into one or two. I tried to fight shy of them, but grizzlies don't appreciate good manners.''

Lou had laughed at his joke, but she wasn't laughing now as the ponderous tread of enormous paws grew closer, ever closer. The bear was so near, she could hear the heavy breaths it took, like the working of a bellows in a blacksmith's shop. She had a fair idea of where it was, but the darkness shrouded it in a stygian mantle her eyes couldn't pierce.

Her every impulse was to rise, to flee. But outrunning a grizzly was as improbable as outrunning a horse. Which was how fast grizzlies could move when they wanted to.

Besides which, Lou wasn't in any condition for a life-and-death race. She hadn't regained full use of her arm, and the agony in her side had yet to abate. Petrified, she listened to the shuffling, wheezing bear, mortally afraid it would catch her scent.

As if it had read her thoughts, the grizzly abruptly stopped and sniffed. Not once, but repeatedly. She tried to convince herself it smelled the mare, not her, and that at any moment it would wander off on the mare's trail and leave her be. But the sniffing went on and on, and there was no denying why. It knew she was there, somewhere. It just hadn't pinpointed her yet.

The prospect of being eaten by a grizzly churned Louisa's innards. She imagined its ghastly fangs shearing through her soft flesh, imagined the bear gulping great chunks of her with zestful enthusiasm.

Oh, Lord! Please let it go away! Lou prayed. But either the Almighty had too many other prayers to answer at that moment or her appeal didn't ascend high enough into the heavens, for the very next moment the grizzly lumbered in her general direction. And now she could see it. A great dark bulk against the vaster darkness of the night, a colossus of might and unrivaled ferocity whose sole purpose in life was to eat,

eat, eat, to devour anything and everything it could catch. It would surely catch her, too, if it located where she was, which it was trying to do by continuing to test the air and swinging its gargantuan head from side to side.

Lou began to tremble uncontrollably, then willed herself to stop. The grizzly's sense of smell was reputed to be far sharper than its eyesight, but the bear was close enough now to detect the slightest movement.

It advanced a few more weighty strides, then tilted its head back, nostrils flaring. A gurgling growl escaped it, as if it were frustrated by its inability to peg where she was.

Maybe the lingering scent of the mare partially masked hers, Lou mused. She saw it lower its nose to the ground and amble back and forth, each step bringing it nearer, steadily nearer. Lou resisted an impulse to scream. Inwardly, she railed at the behemoth, shrieking, *Go away! Go away! Go away!*

The grizzly kept on coming.

Louisa tensed for the inevitable. The bear was going to find her. It was only a matter of time—mere seconds, in fact. She could shoot it, but she'd never heard of an instance where a pistol brought one of the shaggy titans down. All that would do was make it mad. And if a normal griz was hard to kill, a berserk one was unstoppable.

She had to flee. There was no other alternative. Lou rose onto the balls of her feet. Wedging her pistols more firmly under her belt, she braced her hands on the ground for extra leverage. She could smell the bear now, smell its beastly, musty scent, like that of a rug left out in the rain. She could see the dull glint of its fathomless eyes as they swung toward her. And she knew, instinctively knew, that the bear had found her at last.

Instantly, Lou rose, spun, and ran for her life. She ignored her tingling arm, her hurting side. She ignored a muscle spasm in her left leg, a spearing pang in her shoulder. She *must* run or she would die. It was as simple as that. Whipping around a pine to put it between them, Lou pumped her legs in a flurry, speeding recklessly on into the forest. A boulder had to be avoided, a log vaulted. She had gone twenty yards before she mustered the courage to glance over her shoulder. With every fiber of her being she prayed the bear had not given chase, but once again her prayer fell on deaf divine ears.

The grizzly was barreling after her, pacing itself, its huge shoulders and hump rippling with dynamic power apparent even in the dim light.

"Oh, God!"

Lou redoubled her effort, flying along as if she were about to take wing. Her chest ached worse than ever. Fear was part of the reason. Fear so potent, it pulsed through her very veins and threatened to dash all rational thought on the rocks of sheer panic. But she must keep her wits about her! Her wits were her sole edge. For although the grizzly was massively strong, it was no smarter than a cow. Its gut ruled its every waking moment, not its brain.

But then, when that gut was housed in a steely body capable of destroying anything that lived, of what need was a keen intellect? The grizzly knew what it wanted—her—and it was coming after her with the single-minded determination of its kind.

How long Lou ran, she couldn't say. She marveled that the bear didn't overtake her right away, and suspected it was in no great hurry because it believed it had her dead to rights, as it were. It was taking its sweet time, waiting for her to collapse. Then it would finish her off at its leisure.

Suddenly Lou stumbled. She cried out as she pitched forward, her outflung hand preventing total disaster. Heaving upright, she continued to run, run, run. Almost at her heels now was the grizzly. Its breaths were loud in her ears, drowning out her own.

The thump-thump-thump of its paws matched the tempo of her thudding feet. Her skin crawled in expectation of being rent by granite teeth.

Louisa thought of Zach and wished things had turned out differently. She had been looking forward to being his wife, to partaking of the heady nectar of unbridled love, to having children and rearing a family and growing old together. It had been the grandest dream of her life, and now it would never be. Cruel Fate had decreed that her days would end shy of her twentieth birthday. Her marker would be a bleached pile of bones lost amid vast woodland somewhere deep in the Rocky Mountains.

To die was horrible enough. To die never knowing bliss as Zach's wife was horror beyond horror. Never again to feel his tender touch. Never to experience the rapture of delicious passion. Never to be made whole in the mutual union of genuine love.

Another boulder had to be skirted. Lou's legs were flagging despite the dictates of her will. She had gone about as far as she could go. Soon she would be completely spent, completely at the grizzly's mercy.

Lou gave wing to her third and final prayer, a petition that wherever Zach was, he might somehow know her dying thoughts were of him. That on the threshold of meeting her Maker, she was thinking of the greatest gift her Maker had ever granted her. "Oh, how I loved you!" she squandered precious breath saying.

The end was near. Lou's legs were wobbly, her whole body shaking. Another ten feet was all she could manage. But as she fell to her knees, with doom incarnate almost upon her, she gripped both flintlocks. Lou refused to die meekly, to be slaughtered like a lamb or calf. She would resist as best she was able, and if it was a losing cause, so be it. She could perish knowing she had given her all.

Jerking the two pistols, Louisa twisted to face the silvertip.

*   *   *

"I'm awful sorry, son. My big mouth almost got you killed. I just wasn't thinkin' straight."

"I know," Zach answered Ben Frazier. "I don't hold it against you."

They were by themselves, nearer the horses than the fire but still close enough for the two men keeping watch, Frank and Billy Batson, to keep an eye on them. Zach had shifted position so his wrists were behind him, and he was frantically striving to loosen the loops enough to slip the rope off.

"I've always liked your pa," the trapper commented. "An honorable man, Nate King. Worth a hundred of these bastards." Frazier swept the sleepers with a gaze that sizzled with contempt. "It's real comfortin' to know he's out there keepin' an eye on us."

Zach kept the truth to himself. One of the Batsons might overhear. And only so long as the band believed his pa was shadowing them would they let him go on living. "How are you holding up?" he said, changing the subject.

"Not too shabby, all things considered," Frazier said. "That pemmican and water did wonders." Grimacing, he eased onto his back. "But I hurt like the dickens where that snake in the grass poked me with his pigsticker. And I have enough bruises to last me a month of Sundays."

"You've stopped bleeding?"

"Near as I can tell. A little seeps out from time to time, but not enough to fuss about. I'll live. Don't worry."

"Only until you show them where the gold is."

Frazier scrunched up his mouth as if he'd bitten into a lemon. "It galls me to think they might end up rich at my expense. I almost wish there really were Utes hereabouts just so these scum would be wiped out."

A check of the Batsons showed Zach that Billy was fiddling with the fire and Frank was half dozing. Neither was the least bit interested in what the trapper or he had to say. Just to be safe, Zach leaned to one side and whispered, "How far do we have to go?"

Lowering his voice, Frazier responded, "Truth is, I could get us there by sunset tomorrow if I tried. But I plan to take longer. Say, by noon the day after tomorrow. These greeners ain't likely to realize I've hoodwinked 'em. Between the whole bunch, they ain't as smart as a box of rocks."

"You're taking a chance, though."

"What else would you have me do? The faster we get there, the sooner we die. And being dead ain't exactly high on my list of things to do. Somehow, I'm hopin' we can turn the tables on these scalawags before we reach Gold Mountain." Frazier grinned. "Your pa should help in that regard. He's done more than his share of scrappin' with hostiles and such, so he'll likely think of a way to get us out of this tight spot we're in."

Zach wanted to explain the real situation but couldn't.

"I reckon this is what I get for being neighborly," Frazier lamented. "I should've gone on about my own business instead of helpin' this bunch out. But that's how the hog bladder bounces."

The crunch of grass underfoot caused Zach and the trapper to fall silent. Billy Batson, rifle cradled in his arms, hunkered and waited for them to speak. When neither did, Billy said quietly, "I only came over to warn you. Mr. Kendrick said we weren't to let you do any talking. That if you did, we were to kick your teeth in."

Frazier spat on the ground. "And you do whatever he says, right? Slinkin' around his boots like a suck-egg hound! You ought to be ashamed of yourself! You and your brother, both."

The young man looked toward the prone figures. "Keep your voice down!" he whispered. "Wake Mr. Kendrick and there'll be hell to pay."

"Go stand in the fire," Frazier said gruffly. "As if

we give a damn about him or you. You're small and yellow and few to the pod, boy. I hope your pa didn't live long enough to see how you turned out. Or are you a slice off the same bacon?''

"Leave my pa out of this,'' Billy declared. "He's the best man who ever lived. And he was dead set against Frank and me joining this brigade.''

The trapper was about to make another comment that might anger the young farmer, so Zach quickly said, "Don't take it personal. You can't hardly blame us for being short-tempered. Wouldn't you be, in our moccasins?''

Billy nodded. "I'm sorry, for both of you. Were it up to me, I'd let you go. But Mr. Kendrick is top dog here, and anyone who bucks him is asking for grief.''

Frazier puffed out his cheeks in irritation. "Your boss is evil through and through. And if you go on fetchin' sticks for him, you've got as bad a case of the simples as that Pharaoh at the Red Sea.''

"I don't have any choice.''

"Were you behind a door when brains were passed out? A man always has a choice, young fella. He may not like what they are. But doing right or wrong is for us to decide. Then we have to stand by our convictions, or our decisions ain't worth a shovelful of chicken tracks. Don't blame Kendrick for your own shortcomings.''

"You don't mince words, do you, old man?''

"Truth is the truth, whether it's minced, diced, or hard-boiled. Every man has to skin his own skunk. Ain't no gettin' around it.''

Billy Batson's head drooped. "I just can't believe it's gotten to this point. We were all set to head home, then my brother came down sick. If he hadn't, we'd of been miles out on the prairie when you came along.''

"Wishful thinkin' doesn't keep the creek from risin'. Question is, are you man enough to help us? Will you give in to Kendrick or your conscience?''

72

"I'd like to help," Billy reiterated. "But—" A cough by one of the sleepers made him jump. "I've said too much. If I'm caught, there's no telling what Mr. Kendrick will do to me. I'm afraid the two of you are on your own."

"Well, I tried," Frazier said as the younger man rejoined his brother.

"We should have been nicer," Zach said.

"We? You mean me. What would you have me do? Beg for his help? I'm too ornery and proud to bend my knee to any man."

"Being proud is one thing. Being dead is another."

"Hrrmmph" was all the trapper said, and he lapsed into moody reflection.

Zach had a lot to think about, too. Foremost was Louisa. She had been on her own before, so he wasn't unduly concerned. So long as she stayed away from the whites, she would be all right. But knowing her as well as he did, Zach expected her to attempt a rescue. While part of him was pleased beyond measure she would risk her life for his, he was worried she would be caught.

He concentrated on freeing himself. Pain spiked his wrists, growing worse when he rubbed so much skin off, he started bleeding. At the rate he was going, he would rub them raw before he made any headway. But it couldn't be helped. He must escape on his own before Louisa put her life in jeopardy.

Hour by hour the fire dwindled, but it wasn't allowed to go out. Howls and snarls rose on all sides of the bluff, some sounding vaguely human. At one point Zach thought he heard a horse whinny, but he chalked it up to a quirk of the stiff wind.

The Batson brothers were relieved by Cyrus Walton and Elden Johnson. Johnson sat with his blanket over his shoulders, yawning and shaking his head to stay awake. Cyrus Walton stretched, then walked over, asking sarcastically, "Are you two behaving yourselves?"

"Go to hell," Frazier said.

"Most of us do," Walton quipped. "But I think you'll get there a lot sooner than me, old man. Give my regards to his infernal majesty."

Since antagonizing the pudgy clerk wasn't in their best interests, Zach spoke up before Frazier could. "What about that little talk we had earlier today?"

"What about it?"

"Don't beat around the bush. Will you or won't you?"

"Help you?" Walton placed the stock of his rifle on the ground and leaned on the barrel. "You must be joking. The way I see it, the situation has changed considerably."

"How so?"

"You lied to me. There aren't a slew of Utes. There's just one fella. Your father. Against seven armed men who are ready for him. I don't think I have anything to lose by siding with Vince and the boys."

"You're wrong," Zach said. "He'll kill all of you if you don't let us go." Any deception was called for if it saved Louisa.

"*Us* now, is it? The old geezer too? So you can steal his gold instead of us?" Walton smirked. "Forget it, King. You almost pulled the wool over my eyes once. Never again."

"Is the gold worth dying for?"

Cyrus Walton chortled. "You never give up, do you? But since you asked, I'll tell you. Yes, it is. Each of us will go home with enough to last us the rest of our lives. Whatever we want will be ours for the taking. A life of ease and luxury is at our fingertips, and you want me to give it up for *you*?"

"Ease and luxury," Frazier said gloomily. "I thought the same thing once. And look where it's got me."

"You'd still feel that way, old-timer, if we didn't have the upper hand." The pudgy man moved off, beaming cheerfully.

Frazier lay back and closed his eyes. "I should have known it was too good to be true. Nothin' has ever worked out right for me. Since the day I was born, bad luck has sat on my shoulder like a pet raven."

Zach resumed rubbing his wrists up and down. "Don't tell me you're giving up?"

The trapper averted his face.

It didn't matter. Zach wasn't about to admit defeat. His pa had raised him to believe that where there was a will, there was a way. He *would* escape—even if he had to scrape his arms down to the bone.

Chapter Six

The grizzly wasn't there.

Dumbfounded, Louisa May Clark gaped at the empty blackness. She blinked a few times, not believing the evidence of her own eyes. Moments before it had been so close behind her, its fetid breath was on her neck. So where was it now? She looked right and left, but all she saw were trees and more trees.

The bear had vanished off the face of the earth.

Lou rotated, thinking that maybe it had somehow circled around and was coming up on her from the rear. But no, there were only a small boulder and some weeds. Bewildered, she lowered the pistols but didn't let down the hammers. Not yet. Not until she was absolutely sure.

Straining her ears, Lou heard rustling off to the west, then a scratching sound that took her a minute to identify. It was the grizzly, scratching a trunk. "Bear trees" the mountain men called them, boles scarred by claw and teeth marks. Some thought bears did it to sharpen their claws; others were of the opinion it was their way of marking their territory.

Lou was incredulous. The grizzly had just up and left? Without rending her limb from limb? Not that she was disappointed, but if the bear hadn't intended to devour her, why had it chased her?

Then Lou remembered the time two mountain men had strayed into her pa's camp, and the three had sat around jawing until the wee hours. Naturally, the subject of wild animals came up, and naturally, bears were discussed. One of the mountaineers mentioned how fickle they were. How a grizzly might attack someone it stumbled on one day, but run from another person the very next. "They're mighty temperamental," the mountain man had said. "Almost as changeable as womenfolk."

The other visitor had related how once he was pursued by a crusty bruin that trapped him in a narrow ravine. He figured he was a goner, but all the bear had done was sniff him a few times, then waltz off. "Maybe he didn't like how I smelled. I wasn't due for my annual washin' for another couple of months."

The remark was meant as a joke, but maybe there was some truth to it. Grizzlies were "all nose and no brain," according to most folks, so maybe that explained why they would attack one person but not another.

Lou waited, her heart aflutter, fearing the beast's return. She should run, but she was too exhausted. The scritch-scritch-scritch of the bear's claws went on and on. When the noise stopped, Lou's pulse quickened. She was afraid that now the silvertip would finish what it had started. She raised her flintlocks, peering into the murk to catch sight of the gigantic frame that would soon materialize. Only, it didn't. Five minutes of quiet convinced her the griz had wandered off.

Lou sank onto her side and shook as if having a fit, a reaction, she figured, from nearly being eaten. Her jangled nerves were a long time composing themselves. When she was herself again, she lay still, savoring what it felt like to simply be alive.

She was amazed at how clean and pure the air smelled, at how clear and crisp the sounds were, at how soothing it was to be caressed by the northwesterly breeze, at how marvelous it felt to do something as ordinary as inhale and exhale. Too much of life was taken for granted.

"Thank you, God," Lou breathed, and regretfully sat up. She had a lot to do before daylight if she was to save Stalking Coyote.

How strange, Lou thought, that she liked his Shoshone name so much better than his given name. Especially in light of what happened to her father. She would have thought it would be the other way around.

Shrugging, Lou hiked to the south. Her pa had taught her how to navigate at night by locating the Big Dipper and using it as a point of reference to find the North Star. Once she knew where that was, figuring direction was easy. All she had to do was face the North Star and extend her arms. To the right was east, to the left was west, and to the rear was south. Child's play.

Lou's relief at being spared by the bear was short-lived. The griz had been one of many that were abroad, their grunts and growls adding to the general din; painters screeched like women in labor, wolves never stopped uttering plaintive wails, coyotes yipped like lost souls. The bestial bedlam made her feel so small, so insignificant, as if she were a tasty morsel just waiting to be eaten.

The pistols never left her hands. Lou never knew, but a predator might rear out of the shadows, giving her only seconds to react.

She tried to remember landmarks, specific trees and boulders she had passed, but her whole being had been focused on saving her hide, not on the scenery. For the life of her, she couldn't recall anything that stood out.

Lou tried not to dwell on the loss of the rifles and

the horses, but she couldn't help doing so. Being stranded in the mountains meant almost certain death. Even if the stranded person knew how to live off the land, finding water and game were a challenge. She'd heard of one man who was forced to eat rotten meat from a buffalo carcass, of another who had taken to a diet of grass and leaves. Both survived, but barely.

Lou had the added worry of Stalking Coyote. His life was in her hands. She and only she could rescue him. Without a mount, though, it couldn't be done. The man she loved might well die because she had been unable to control a spooked horse.

Anxiety and guilt hastened her footsteps, and for over an hour, by her reckoning, Lou searched and searched, without result. No horses, no rifles, nothing. Worse, she thought the bluff should be visible, but whenever a gap in the trees permitted her to scour the countryside, it was nowhere to be seen.

Despair enfolded her heart in crushing claws. *She was lost!* She had gotten so turned around during the mare's mad dash and her own flight that she was nowhere near where she thought she should be.

Lou bit her lower lip to keep from crying. Now wasn't the time for tears. What was it Nate King once remarked? ''The secret to staying alive in the wilds is to keep your wits about you. Panic will kill you quicker than a rattler's bite. Always think things through. Learn from your mistakes. And whatever you do, never give up.''

Easy for him to say, Lou thought. He wasn't the one all alone, adrift in a boundless sea of forest and grass. He wasn't the one surrounded on all sides by vicious meat-eaters, or the one who would never forgive herself if anything happened to the man she cherished more than she did her own life.

Louisa May Clark stopped and turned moist eyes to the heavens. She had prayed for a miracle once and it had been granted. Maybe she should pray for another.

* * *

A foot in the ribs woke up Zach King shortly before dawn. A brisk tang to the air helped dispel some of the bitterness in his mouth. Bitterness caused by his inability to free himself during the night. He had tried and tried, rubbing his wrists until they were covered with blood. Yet the rope never slackened.

Then Zach had pried at the knots, but they were corded like bands of metal. He couldn't undo a single one.

Toward four in the morning his arms had drooped and his fingers had been too sore to move. Zach had fought to stay awake, but his body succumbed to the abuse he'd endured, to the lack of rest and food. Against his will he had drifted into dreamland, sleeping fitfully, plagued by nightmares he couldn't recollect when he awoke.

Now, rubbing his eyes, Zach sat up. The members of the so-called brigade were up and about, but as sluggish as snails in cold weather. Ed Stark, stamping his feet next to the fire, was his usual friendly self. "You're lucky, 'breed. I wanted to cut you to wake you up, but Vince said he didn't want you bleeding all day."

Kendrick was shaking Ben Frazier, who was slow to respond. Annoyed, the big man smacked the trapper, not once but twice, and Frazier snapped up in alarm, his cheek bright red. "What? What is it?"

"Rise and shine, old man. You've got until sunset tonight to show us where the gold is, or by tomorrow morning you'll be missing a few fingers and toes."

Frazier recovered his wits quickly. "I never told you we'd get there by then. It might be tomorrow sometime."

Grinning smugly, Kendrick straightened. "That soon? Hell, for all I knew, it would've taken a week. You never said until now."

Cyrus Walton laughed. "Nice going, Vince. You sure skunked the old fart."

The greenhorns were in high spirits, and why shouldn't

they be? They were going to be wealthy. Judging by their dreamy expressions, they were contemplating what they would do with their ill-gotten riches. Even the Batson brothers. Billy commented that he couldn't wait to see his pa's face when they bought him a new plow.

"A *plow*?" Ed Stark cackled. "You could wind up with enough money to start your own bank, and all you can think of is to buy your pa a stinking plow?"

"What's wrong with that?" Billy asked defensively.

"Nothing at all. Once a hick, always a hick, I reckon."

Zach flinched as he stiffly pushed upward. His forearms were leaden, his wrists layered with dry blood. But it was thirst that bothered him the most. It had been a full day since he last drank anything, and his mouth and throat were parched. Seeing Ira Sanders upend the water skin, he asked, "Any chance I could have some?"

"Not on your life, 'breed," Ed Stark said.

Kendrick was picking up his saddle. "Lick the dew off the grass. That ought to hold you until you die."

Several of the whites thought their leader was hilarious. Billy Batson frowned but didn't have the gumption to protest.

Ben Frazier surprised everyone by declaring, "Give the boy some water, Kendrick. Or no gold."

The big man was about to hoist his rig onto his mount. "No one tells me what to do. Ever."

"Call it a swap. My cooperation in return for doing me a favor."

"You old coot. You'll cooperate whether you want to or not. Haven't you got that through that thick noggin of yours yet?"

Frazier folded his arms and stiffened his spine. "Do your worst. I've had a belly full of your threats."

All eyes were on Kendrick as he threw his saddle on his sorrel. Pivoting, he was on the trapper in two bounds. He gripped the little finger on Frazier's left hand, drew his butcher knife, and pressed the edge against it. "Did you think I was bluffing? One more word out of you and you can say good-bye to your pinkie."

Frazier wasn't intimidated. "Go ahead. I dare you."

"No!" Zach yelled. "Don't lose a finger on my account. It's not worth it."

Support came from an unlikely source. Elden Johnson, of all people, put a hand on Kendrick's shoulder. "Let him be, Vince. You'll be sorry if you don't."

No one was more astounded than Kendrick. "What in hell's gotten into you? Taking this flea-ridden bastard's side against me? I'd expect it from some of the others, but you and I always see eye to eye."

"It's in our own best interests not to touch him."

"Did that wallop on the head scramble your marbles? How do you figure?"

Johnson rattled off the reasons. "He's already weak from loss of blood. Cut off a finger or two and he'll lose a lot more. He might even become so weak, he can't guide us to the gold. Do you want that?" Not waiting for a reply, he went on. "Either way, he sure won't be in any shape to ride. Maybe not for days. Longer if infection sets in. Do you want that?" Johnson answered his own question. "No, of course you don't. None of us do. The sooner we get this over with, the safer we'll be. So do as he wants. Give the half-breed a few sips. What can it hurt?"

Kendrick released Frazier and stood. "You always were the real brains of this bunch. All right. Let the 'breed have a little." He abruptly whirled on the trapper. "But don't get any wrong notions, old-timer. I'm not backing down. You haven't won."

" 'Course I haven't," Frazier gloated.

The water was some of the tastiest Zach ever swallowed. Each sip was a luxury, each swallow a testament to life itself. Johnson took the water skin away much too soon, but Zach had slaked his thirst enough to get by.

Walton and Sanders threw Zach over a packhorse. He requested they untie his ankles so he could ride upright, but they only snickered and regarded him as if his brains had seeped out his ears.

"Hope you have a tinplate gut, 'breed," Ira Sanders said. "Ten hours of bouncing around on it will about do you in."

It was more like ten minutes. In no time at all, Zach's stomach was being lanced by pain whenever the packhorse moved any faster than a walk. For the longest while he felt sick, but the feeling faded. He counted on the brigade stopping for half an hour or so at midday to rest the horses, but Kendrick was too filled with greed to delay for more than ten minutes. And no one bothered to take Zach off.

By three o'clock Zach was in such anguish, he thought he would scream. But then something strange occurred. The pain lessened on its own. He couldn't say why. Maybe his nerve endings had taken all the punishment they could, and shut down. Maybe his mind was numbed by the ordeal. Or maybe he just didn't care anymore.

The sun arced westward. Frazier kept telling Kendrick that Gold Mountain was "just up yonder," but they never reached it. Zach doubted they would before the sun sank. What would Kendrick do? Carry out his threat?

Wait and see was the only thing to do.

The bearded rider came out of woods to the east, astride a splendid bay that once was the proud possession of a Flathead warrior. In his hair he wore an eagle feather, Cheyenne-fashion. But his beaded buckskins and moccasins were Shoshone, and the parfleches strapped to his saddle were decorated with Shoshone designs. His features, though, were those of a white man—as were the striking green eyes that surveyed his world.

Every now and again he would bend to inspect the tracks he paralleled.

Large of build, he had broad shoulders that would be the envy of many. A mane of hair fell to those shoulders, crowned by a beaver hat. As with most of his kind, he was a living armory, with a rifle, pistols, and long knife—and a tomahawk obtained during his wide-flung travels.

He could pass for an Indian if he wanted, so bronzed and weathered were his rugged features.

The rider's forehead creased when he came to where the pair he was after had dismounted on top of a ridge. He did the same, his eagle gaze probing a small valley below and settling on a clearing in some trees. The charred remains of a campfire stood out like the proverbial sore thumb.

"So," he said aloud to himself. "Strangers."

The bay took the slope on its hindquarters, its forelegs rigid. When only twenty feet from the bottom it slipped and slid and would have fallen if not for the superb mastery of the man in the saddle.

Undaunted, the rider did not even slow down. At the tree line, he spurred the bay on.

Rosy sunbeams bathed the clearing, lending it a deceptive, peaceful aspect. An aspect that never fooled the horseman. When he dismounted, he had his Hawken in hand. As he crisscrossed the clearing, he never took his eyes off the woods for very long.

Most anyone else would have been befuddled by the confusing jumble of footprints and hoofprints. But not the frontiersman. He read them with the same ease literate people read books, able to tell one track from another by characteristics most would never detect. By the end of half an hour he knew there had been eight men in the party, and that all eight, in the company of one of those he sought, had ridden westward.

Pieces of rope at the base of a tree hinted something

was amiss. Sinking onto a knee, the bearded rider discovered smears of blood on the ground and drops on the bole. The prints of the unfortunate involved, toes splayed outward, told him it had been a white man.

A white being tortured by other whites.

Therein was a mystery that grew in scope when the rider found where only one of those he was after had entered the clearing. On foot, no less. He backtracked to learn why, and what he found brought him back to the clearing for a second, more thorough examination.

The bay was chomping at the bit when the frontiersman swung up and hauled on the reins. Thunder and lightning danced on his brow as he brought his mount to a gallop. Someone had a lot to answer for. They would pay dearly should any harm befall his son.

Very dearly indeed.

It was the gay chirping of a robin that brought Louisa May Clark back to the world of the living. Squinting against the bright sun, she rose, furious at herself for oversleeping. Fatigue had ended her search the night before, fatigue so potent, she had been asleep the moment her cheek touched the ground. An early riser by nature, she'd figured she would wake up about dawn. But the sun was several hours high.

Lou smacked her lips, then ran a hand through her hair. She was hungry, grungy, and aching, and she would give anything for a hot bath.

Arching her back, Lou stretched. Spying the bluff, not a quarter of a mile to the southwest, shocked her fully awake. She jogged toward it, her leg muscles objecting to every step. At the talus slope she was stunned to see the game trail, plain as day. How she could have missed it the night before, she would never know.

Lou scrambled upward, using her hands in her haste to reach the top. As she had feared, Kendrick's bunch were long gone, her darling Zach with them.

But if it was true that fortune smiled on those who

had nothing to smile about, then twice in twelve hours a miracle had taken place. For grazing near the smoldering embers of the fire was Stalking Coyote's dun. It had scaled the bluff on its own, maybe drawn by Zach's scent, maybe lured by the scent of other horses.

Ecstatic, Lou approached slowly, afraid it would run off if she wasn't careful. "Ho there, horse," she coaxed. It didn't have a name. Stalking Coyote refused to give it one, saying that wasn't the Shoshone way. "You remember me, don't you? Sure you do. I've fed you enough carrots to gag a goat."

The dun munched contentedly, showing no inclination to run off.

"I've given you sugar when I wasn't supposed to," Louisa mentioned. "I've taken you to the lake to drink." Another few steps and her hand fell on the bridle. Overjoyed, she hugged the horse, then grasped the saddle to pull herself up. The dun was much larger than the mare, a full sixteen hands, and she had to hook her foot in the stirrup to lever her legs high enough to straddle its broad back.

Recalling the pemmican Stalking Coyote carried in a parfleche, Lou fumbled at the tie, opened it, and pulled out a bundle wrapped in rabbit skin. Fingers fumbling, she removed a piece and hungrily bit down. Her stomach leaped upward as if to meet the food halfway, then growled as loud as the grizzly had. She chewed slowly, relishing the taste, the texture, the feel.

"What am I doing?" Lou abruptly asked herself. Here she was, wasting time, while with every second that elapsed the distance between Stalking Coyote and her widened.

"Let's go, horse." A slap of Lou's hand was enough to goad the dun into a trot. She felt rejuvenated, due more to the horse than the food. Now she stood a very good chance of overtaking the cutthroats before dark, especially if they stopped to rest now and then, as they were bound to do.

"Hang on, darling. I'm coming for you!" Lou declared. She didn't mind talking to herself. She had done so long before she met Zach. Solitude was to blame, the many hours spent alone when her pa was off checking traps and raising plews. As he'd once said, "The best listeners are our own ears."

The daunting task she faced did nothing to dampen Lou's zeal. She would save her prince—or she would die trying.

"A couple of hours more and the sun will set."

The thinly veiled threat in the announcement by Vince Kendrick wasn't lost on any of the men strung out behind him, particularly Ben Frazier. No one had objected to the trapper riding next to Zach, which he had been doing most of the afternoon.

"Hear that, sonny? It was for my benefit. He thinks he can scare me, the blamed mooncalf."

"Don't prod him. Please."

"I'm touched you care," Frazier said. "But I ain't about to tread lightly. I've had my fill of him, actin' as if he's the greatest thing since the chamber pot."

They traveled several hundred more yards, then the column reined up. Kendrick and Ed Stark were off their mounts, and Stark was bent low over the grass as if he had dropped something and was hunting for it.

"Cyrus!" Kendrick bellowed. "Bring the half-breed!"

Walton tugged on the lead rope.

The trapper tagged along, winking at Zach and joking, "Where you go, I go. Just in case one of these possum heads takes a notion to do you harm."

Clods of earth had been torn up in a fifteen-yard-wide strip. "What do you make of all these tracks, 'breed?" Kendrick demanded.

Zach had a bird's-eye view. A low-flying bird, admittedly, yet that made studying the finer details of the hoofprints a snap. But some of the trapper's feistiness had worn off on him. "Why ask me?"

"Don't give me any guff. Everyone knows Injuns learn to track before they learn to talk. What do you make of all this?"

Frazier broke in. "Hell, I can tell you what you want to know. Fifteen to twenty unshod horses came by here less than two hours ago, travelin' north. Utes, would be my guess."

The others were gathering around, and they weren't happy at the news. "Utes?" Cyrus Walton said. "Real Utes this time?"

Kendrick shrugged. "So what? It's a hunting party, heading for their village. Nothing for us to lose any sleep over."

Zach craned his head high enough to see the one he would most love to count coup on. "You're mistaken. Utes live south of here. When they hunt, they usually go east, toward the prairie. For buffalo. This must be a war party, on a raid. And they'll be back this way in a few days. When they cross our trail, they'll come after us."

"You're just guessing," Kendrick said. "It could be a month before they return. Or they could go another way."

Frazier tittered. "I'd give up on the gold, were I you. It ain't worth havin' more arrows stuck in you than a porcupine has quills."

"He has a point," Frank Batson said. "The last thing we want is to tangle with bucks out to add to their scalp collection."

"Who held an election and voted you the new boss?" Kendrick demanded. "I liked you better when you were too sick to flap your gums." Climbing back on his horse, he gestured. "We're seeing this through together. And I'll gladly shoot the first bastard who tries to run out on us."

Zach sagged against the packhorse, then snapped his head up again. Had it been his imagination, or had he seen a solitary warrior on a hill to the northwest?

When he looked the second time, the man was gone. Chalking it up to lack of sleep and food, Zach didn't rate it worth mentioning.

The gold seekers resumed their journey.

Chapter Seven

Louisa May Clark didn't see the bear until almost too late.

Ironically, she suspected it was the same grizzly that had chased her the night before. It lay in a basin rife with high grass, sleeping, when she blundered onto it. She had decided to let the dun rest awhile and veered toward a stand of trees, where they would lie low for half an hour. Partway there, she saw the bowl-shaped depression and the enormous brown mass lying at the bottom. The distinctive hump warned her what it was, and she wheeled the dun to flee.

But the harm had been done. The silvertip had been awakened, and it charged up out of the basin in a surly mood. To put it mildly. Slavering and snarling, it bore down on her like a bull gone amok.

Lou raced westward. She was confident the dun could outrun the monster. But what if Kendrick's bunch had stopped not far ahead and she blundered on them as she had the bear? There would go any chance she had of saving Stalking Coyote. So Lou cut to the right, to the northwest, and lashed the reins against the dun's neck for an extra spurt of speed.

It was well she did. The grizzly put on a spurt of its own. In a twinkling it was upon her, a huge forepaw flicking at the dun's flanks. Instead of rending flesh, the claws clipped the dun's bobbing tail.

At the contact, the dun shot forward, gaining a small lead but a lead nonetheless. And any lead was better than none when the alternative was to go down under the grinding teeth and rending claws of a living engine of destruction.

Lou thought the bear would soon give up. It was common knowledge grizzlies did not have a great deal of stamina. They could run fast, but only for short distances. Then they tired. Everyone said so.

But after a minute of harrowing pursuit, Lou began to question conventional wisdom. Because the grizzly showed no signs of tiring and giving up. If anything, it was going faster, incensed by its failure to overtake her. Drool rained over its lower lip as its paws chewed up the ground like living rakes.

"Go, horse, go!" Lou urged, knowing it couldn't possibly make the dun run any swifter but needing to voice her anxiety anyway.

Ahead woodland appeared. Lou's breath caught in her throat; it would slow her down! She couldn't maintain the same pace in the thick of densely pressed trees and brush. The bear would catch up, would bring the dun crashing to earth. And if she tried to change direction again before she got there, with the beast right on her heels, it would be all be over in seconds.

She had to slow it down somehow. Glancing back, she placed a hand on a flintlock.

At that juncture the grizzly did slow, growling hideously as if calling her every cussword in the grizzly vocabulary.

Louisa smiled and waved and then was in the trees. Bringing the dun to a halt, she twisted in the saddle to confirm the behemoth had lost interest. It had already turned and was shuffling southward, its great head swinging from side to side. It reminded her so much of a grumpy old man that she laughed.

"You were lucky, boy, is all."

Startled, Louisa swung around, palming the pistol and cocking it as she drew. Not twenty feet away, on a tired-looking horse, sat a tired-looking man in his early thirties, dressed in buckskins that had seen better days. Straggly hair and a straggly beard lent him the image of a wild man, but his smile was kindly and he made no move to use his rifle or flintlocks. Behind him was a packhorse laden with traps and a small pile of peltries. "I didn't know you were there, mister!" Lou blurted.

"Of course you didn't. You had your hands full with that griz." The man kneed his horse closer. "Name's Bartholomew Dunne, sonny. Earlier I spotted a war party northwest of here and managed to slip on by them. But I figured it'd be smart to lay low and was resting up when you came along. What might your handle be?"

The man was friendly enough. "Lou," she answered. "Lou Clark."

"Right pleased to make your acquaintance." Bartholomew scratched his beard. "Betwixt bears and Indians, it isn't hardly healthy for white folks hereabouts."

"A war party, you say?" Lou envisioned her beloved falling into their clutches.

"Utes, most likely. Mind you, I didn't go up and ask. But their faces and horses were painted. And unless you're a greener, you must know what that means."

"A war party, sure enough," Louisa agreed. She eased down the hammer and slid the pistol under her belt.

Bartholomew stared past her, then to the east. "What in God's name are you doing all by yourself, boy? If you don't mind my sayin' so, you're a mite young and a mite puny to be traipsing around by your lonesome.''

No one liked to be called "puny." "I can take care of myself," Lou responded. "And I'm not by myself. I'm trying—" She stopped, about to say "to save the man I'm going to marry." Instead, she finished with "—to catch up with the trapping brigade I belong to. I was separated from them this morning."

"A trapping brigade?" Bartholomew Dunne chuckled. "Damnation. You are greeners. The days of the brigades are over, boy. Haven't you heard?"

"We'll do all right," Lou hedged.

"Like hell. The beaver are plumb trapped out. I should know. I've been a trapper for going on nigh ten years." Bartholomew grew wistful. "When I came to the Rockies, there were beaver aplenty. My first season I made over three hundred dollars. And until two or three seasons ago, I was still making fairly good money. But then the beaver got harder and harder to find. I had to go farther and farther back into the mountains. Now there's hardly enough left to make a decent rug." He nodded at the peltries on his pack-horse. "Those there are the last of the prime hides."

"Be that as it may, I still have to catch up with my friends." Anxious on Zach's account, Louisa lifted her reins.

"Hold on. What's your rush? They're bound to wait for you, aren't they?"

"They're quite a ways ahead, and I want to rejoin them before dark." Lou didn't mean to be rude, but she wished the man would be off about his own business.

Bartholomew had no such desire. "It's been a coon's age since last I jawed with white men. I'd like to tag along, if you don't mind."

"You would?" Lou would rather he didn't. She'd have to go more slowly than she wanted.

"What's wrong with that? I can save your friends from wasting all their time and energy on a fool's quest. There just aren't any beaver to be had."

To refuse might arouse suspicion. So as much as Lou was against it, she said, "There's nothing wrong. I'm just in a hurry. Come along."

They rode from the trees, Lou masking how upset she was. She noticed Dunne scrutinizing her.

"How old are you, boy, if I can ask without getting your dander up?"

Lou told him.

"You don't say. Why, there's hardly a whisker on your chin. How is it you haven't started to shave yet?"

"Smooth chins run in my family," Louisa said, hoping it wasn't too far-fetched.

"Ah. I knew a family back in Indiana who were that way. The menfolk couldn't grow a decent beard if their lives depended on it. They used to be a laughingstock until they all married some of the prettiest fillies in the county." Bartholomew scratched his beard again. "Beats me why any gal would marry a fella who didn't have a decent head of hair. I'm proud of mine, even if I do have a problem with lice now and then."

Lou made a mental note to not let him get within a foot of her.

"How many men are in this brigade of yours?"

"Nine, counting me." Lou thought of something that might dissuade him from coming along. "What about that war party? Aren't you worried about the Utes?"

"Hell, they're miles off by now. And if they're not, there's safety in numbers. I'm better off with you and your friends."

Lou resigned herself to sharing his company and hurried on. So immersed was she in sweet thoughts of Zach, she didn't pay much attention to her newfound companion. Had she, she would have noticed the many secret glances he cast at her, perplexed glances, probing glances.

They did not bode well.

* * *

A spectacular sunset blazed the western sky when Vince Kendrick raised an arm and brought the line to a halt.

"This is it," Ben Frazier said.

Zach was afraid he agreed, and afraid for the old man. Kendrick had been glaring at the trapper all afternoon, working himself into a funk, and now the dam was about to burst. Zach lifted his head, grimacing at a kink in his neck. Which was the least of his many aches and pains. "Remember. Don't provoke him."

Frazier snorted. "Shows how much you know about human nature, sonny. He made me eat crow, remember? But by gum, he won't make me eat it twice."

"Listen to me. If we work together, we can live through this."

The trapper smiled and said softly, "Damn if you aren't a chip off the old block. Your pa has a reputation for being as honorable a feller as ever lived, and I reckon it must run in the family."

No one had ever compared Zach to his father before. He did not know what to say.

"I always wanted a boy of my own," Frazier said rather sorrowfully. "Had me a Nez Percé woman once, the finest female who ever lived. She talked about havin' sprouts, but before she could get pregnant, the Bloods raided our village and she took an arrow meant for me."

"I'm sorry."

"Such is life," Frazier said. "If it ain't chickens, its feathers."

Kendrick and Stark approached from the head of the column, Johnson and Sanders from the rear.

Zach tried one last time. "Did you ever think that if you let them kill you, they still might find the gold? They're not about to give up. Kendrick will spend years hunting if he has to."

"Now, that would sorely vex me. I'd rather give it

all to a politician than let it fall into the hands of these scum.''

The quartet reined up, and Kendrick waded right in. Leaning on his saddle horn, he said harshly, ''I warned you, old man. I made it plain as could be what would happen if we didn't reach the gold by nightfall.''

''Go ahead, Vince! Cut off a finger,'' Ed Stark coaxed. ''We'll hold him for you.''

Frazier was as calm as a toad in the sun. ''And I made it plain we might not get there today. But since you coyotes are all het up, I might as well break the good news.''

''What are you dithering about?'' Kendrick said.

The trapper pointed. ''See that ridge yonder?''

''What about it?''

''Look past it and tell me what's there.''

Vince Kendrick rose in his stirrups. ''A peak. A small mountain. Is that a landmark?''

''It's Gold Mountain, as I call it. That's where we'll find what you're after.''

Four sets of eyes glinted with greed. ''If you're pulling our leg, old-timer,'' Kendrick said, ''I'll take up where I left off with that brand last night.''

''Unlike some people I can think of,'' Frazier retorted, giving each of them a meaningful stare, ''I've got enough brains to grease a skillet. And being tortured once in my lifetime was enough.''

''Gold Mountain,'' Ed Stark said in awe, then sobered and faced Kendrick. ''Now that we know, what use do we have for gramps here? I say we put a ball between his eyes so we don't have to listen to him jabber anymore.''

''Go right ahead,'' Frazier said glibly. ''But before you do, keep in mind that mountain might look small from here, but up close it's as big as they come. Without knowin' exactly where the gold is, you could search for months and never find it.''

''He has a point,'' Elden Johnson said.

Kendrick had not been listening. He was mesmerized by the peak. "So close, yet so far. But hell. It can't be more than fifteen, twenty miles. If we pushed, we'd be there by the middle of the night."

Johnson turned. "And then what? Climb it in the dark? Stumble around looking for gold we can't see? It's wiser to get a good night's sleep and an early start."

Once again the human anvil's logic couldn't be denied. Kendrick glowered, though, and said, "Have I ever told you how much of a pain in the ass you can be? Don't you ever get tired of always being right?"

"No."

Zach was glad the old man would be spared, but they'd only bought him another day of life, at most. Once the greenhorns had their hands on the gold, they'd have no further use for him.

By then, Zach might be dead himself. This was his second day without food and without much water. He was growing weaker by the hour and would soon be in no shape to escape even if he could shed his bounds.

His plight was growing desperate, his hope waning. He kept looking for sign of Louisa. Even though he didn't want her to endanger herself on his account, she might be his only hope. Where was she? When would she try to free him? If she waited too long he would be too weak to lift a finger, let alone mount a horse. She would sacrifice herself in vain.

Zach couldn't let that happen.

The broad-shouldered frontiersman on the magnificent bay had spied the bluff from a long way off. Soon he would be at its base, and soon thereafter the sun would set and he must stop for the night. It was not to his liking.

The two he sought were in trouble. Its exact nature was a mystery, but irrelevant. When a member of his family was threatened, he would uproot heaven and hell to protect them. As would any man worthy of being a father.

His family was everything to him. Once, he wouldn't have thought so. In the ignorance of his youth, he had put himself before all else and based his decisions on whether they were good or bad for him. Only later, after taking a wife and becoming a husband, did he see that the world wasn't made for his use alone. Having others to think of gave him new insight into the scheme of things, into how caring for those who depended on him was the measure of a man's true worth.

The love a husband showed for his wife, the affection a father showed for children, was a direct reflection on his own nature. A mature man nurtured that love as if it were the most priceless treasure anyone could possess—which it was.

Now two of his own needed him, and he would not fail them.

But then the frontiersman came to a talus slope and saw where the dun and the mare had traveled westward, while the party his pride and joy was with had gone up a game trail to the top.

The mountain man reined up. The tracks revealed that the dun had returned alone. It had been walking slowly and nibbling at every tuft of grass that caught its fancy, which it would only do if it weren't being ridden. Human tracks added to the puzzle. One of those he was after had gone up the slope on foot. Why? What had happened to the mare? He rode on.

Near some boulders the bearded man found where the mare had bolted into the woods. He glanced at the crest, then at the vegetation. "I'd best be sure," he said, and entered the trees.

"You don't want to make a fire?"

Bartholomew Dunne's surprise was warranted. No one ever made a cold camp unless it was absolutely necessary. Such as when hostiles were nearby, or there was no means to set kindling to blaze.

Louisa May Clark didn't want one, because the men

who had taken Stalking Coyote might see it, but she couldn't explain without sparking a hundred and one questions better left unanswered for the time being.

"Why would you want to go without, sonny?" Bartholomew asked. "I have enough coffee and sugar for both of us." He wagged the coffeepot he had taken off his packhorse. "Sure you wouldn't like some?"

"Sure I would," Lou said, "but we can't advertise where we are with an Ute war party in the area."

"Oh, hell. Is that all?" Bartholomew set down the pot. "We'll keep the fire small. No one will spot it."

They had stopped in a dry wash within a stone's throw of the tracks left by Zach's abductors. Their horses were hobbled so no one could make off with them during the night. Lou spread out Zach's saddle blanket for her bed, then helped gather wood.

Dunne had become awful quiet the last hour or so, and twice she caught him giving her strange looks. When they were done, they piled their armloads of dry branches. From his possibles bag Bartholomew took a fire steel and flint, and in short order had a fire going. It gave off little smoke. Even so, he swatted at the slender wisps to disperse them before they rose any higher.

Lou portioned out pemmican for the two of them and gave the man his share.

"I thank you, sonny." Bartholomew chomped off a mouthful, chewed a moment, then said, "A Shoshone made this. Am I right?"

Impressed, Lou asked, "How did you guess?"

"Guessing had nothing to do with it. No two tribes make pemmican exactly the same. Some add more fat, some add different kinds of berries. Some like it sweet, some like it tart."

Dunne chewed some more, staring at her so hard, Lou grew uncomfortable and wouldn't look at him. She wondered if she had made a mistake in letting him join her. Stalking Coyote's pa had warned her many times never to take anyone at face value. And to never trust a soul unless they earned her trust by their actions.

"So, if I'm not snooping, how is it that you got hold of Shoshone pemmican?"

"We ran into a hunting party and they had some to trade," Lou said.

"Friendly devils, those Shoshones. They're one of the few tribes that like whites. Last time I stayed at one of their villages, they went out of their way to make me feel at home."

"They're decent people. Salt of the earth."

Warming to the topic, Bartholomew prattled on with his mouth crammed with pemmican. "So are the Flatheads and the Nez Percé. I can't recollect a single instance where either ever harmed a white. The Crows are friendly, too, but they're also thieving rascals who will steal the clothes off your back and leave you buck naked if they think they can do it and get away with it."

Lou was not aware her cheeks had flushed with color, but they must have, because Dunne gave her a peculiar look.

"What did I say? Why did you blush?"

"Must be the fire," Lou suggested.

"Most likely. Where was I? Oh. The Crows. Years ago they were a lot worse than they are now. Then one day it dawned on them that our guns would come in handy against their old enemies, the Blackfeet. So all of a sudden we became their best friends."

"My soon-to-be father-in-law says that our coming has changed the Indians forever. That even if all the whites in the mountains were to pack up and go home, we can't undo the harm that's been done." Lou figured Bartholomew would ask what kind of harm, but he was more interested in something else.

"You're fixing to get married? When?"

"The date hasn't been set yet."

"What's your gal like?"

Lou hesitated. What would a guy say? What female

traits did men most like to talk about when no women were around? How intelligent they were? Their dispositions? "She's real sweet."

"Sweet?"

"Kind. Nice. Considerate. That kind of sweet." Lou couldn't understand why Dunne chortled.

"That's not exactly what I meant." Bartholomew winked, then raised his hands to his chest and cupped his palms as if he were holding melons. "Does she have udders big enough to use as pillows?"

"I beg your pardon?"

"My Flathead woman did. Lordy, she was a natural wonder."

"I really don't think this is fit to talk about."

"Why not? What harm is there? It's not as if I asked if you've measured them." Bartholomew ripped off more pemmican. "You haven't, have you?"

Lou felt her face grow warm. "I should say not! Gentlemen don't do things like that. And men certainly shouldn't share intimate details about the ladies they love."

"We shouldn't? Since when?"

Lou was irate enough to chuck a stone at him, but she refrained. So this was how men were when alone? Randy satyrs who took boyish delight in talking about sexual matters! Who would have thought it!

Dunne was gazing into the distance, but he was lost in memory. "I remember what I was like at your age. Womenfolk were all I ever thought about. Kissing them, holding them. Smelling them, tasting them. Yes, indeedy, I couldn't get enough."

Lou tried to divert him to a different subject. "Yet you came west to live all alone as a trapper?"

"Sounds scatterbrained, doesn't it? But I'd heard all about Indian women. How they're much more open about sex than whites. And how a man doesn't have to marry one to sleep with her—"

"That's enough."

Bartholomew scratched his beard some more. "Don't

tell me you're one of those prudes who thinks so much as touching a female is wrong? Hellfire, if that were the case, the human race would come to a quick end, wouldn't it?''

Lou refused to dignify his lewd comments with a response. She gazed into the fire, expecting him to take the hint. But he didn't.

''My mother was that way. It always amazed me I was even born. My father must have knocked her out one night so he could take advantage, otherwise I wouldn't be sitting here.'' Dunne laughed. ''People are so contrary. It's a wonder we can even get along.''

''I'm going to turn in,'' Lou announced.

''What? This early?''

''I want to head out at first light,'' Lou explained. ''And I've hardly had any sleep in the past twenty-four hours.'' She had propped Zach's saddle at the edge of the blanket to use as a pillow, and now she turned her back to the trapper and lay down. But not before filling her right hand with a pistol and her left hand with her knife. ''We should take turns standing guard. Wake me when the night's half done.''

''Do you always sleep armed to the teeth?'' Bartholomew asked.

''Yes, and I'm a light sleeper. So when you wake me up, just holler. Don't touch me, or I'm liable to stick you before I know what I'm doing.'' Lou smiled at her fib. Like all the other untruths she had told recently, she had a good excuse.

''Sure, sonny. Whatever you want,'' Bartholomew Dunne said. He swallowed the pemmican but didn't take another bite. Eyebrows knit, he sat and stared across the fire at the lithe figure lying there. A painter screeched, an owl hooted, and a shooting star streaked across the sky, but he paid them no mind. All he did was stare, stare, stare.

Chapter Eight

The trouble started shortly after Kendrick's brigade ate their supper.

Cyrus Walton had shot a doe while out gathering firewood, and soon thereafter a bloody haunch was roasting over a makeshift spit. The greenhorns were in fine spirits, joking and laughing and bantering about all the wonderful things they would buy with their share of the gold.

Zach King and Ben Frazier were pretty much ignored, although at Kendrick's orders both were given water. Zach was thirsty enough to drink all that was left in the water skin, but Elden Johnson yanked it away from his lips after only half a dozen swallows.

Hurting from head to toe, sore and stiff in every muscle and joint, Zach watched the haunch slowly turn on the spit and brown to a well-done sheen. The delicious fragrance made his stomach growl. A constant sharp ache deep in his gut added to his woes. His mouth watered uncontrollably. He had never been so hungry in his life.

When the haunch was done, Ira Sanders sliced off sizable chunks and passed them out. Elden Johnson tore into his piece like a famished wolf, and the sight caused the ache in Zach's gut to worsen. He had to turn away. He looked around when Cyrus Walton brought some to Frazier.

"What about me?"

The pudgy clerk turned to go.

"What about me?" Zach repeated.

Walton grinned. "What about you, 'breed? Vince didn't say anything about feeding you. Starve, for all I care."

Frazier hadn't touched his yet. "Let this boy die and you'll regret it. His pa will wipe out every last one of you miserable worms." Raising his voice, he said, "You hear me, Kendrick? Just like you need me alive to find the gold, you need Zach alive to fend off his pa."

"He's right," Elden Johnson said.

Kendrick was chewing with gusto, his chin smeared with grease and blood. He stared at the trapper, then at Zach, and lastly at Cyrus Walton. "Give the 'breed some, too. As much as I'd love to stake him out and peel his hide off, we'd better play it safe."

So Zach was given meat. And since he couldn't very well eat with his hands bound behind his back, Walton untied the rope. Zach feared the man would see his scraped wrists and the dried blood and inform Kendrick that he had been trying to escape, but Walton never said a thing. Zach's back was turned away from the fire, so maybe Walton didn't notice. Or maybe Walton didn't care, since it was evident Zach's struggles had done little good.

The venison was placed on the grass in front of him. Instantly, Zach went to reach for it, and immediately regretted being hasty. His arms screamed with torment. He nearly did the same out loud. The circulation had been cut off for so long, he couldn't move them. He tried again after a bit, but it was as if his shoulders were fused solid. Even wriggling his fingers was excruciating.

Zach knew he must be patient. Given time, he would be able to pick up the meat. But he couldn't wait. He was too famished. Bending, he bit into the venison where it lay. The taste was exquisite. His belly did flip-flops, and saliva gushed from his mouth. Zach gnawed it like a dog gnawing a bone, then, with a wrench, tore off a savory strip.

"Take your time, son," Frazier cautioned, "or you'll get sick."

Easier said than done. Zach's natural impulse was to down the mouthful in a single gulp. But he willed himself to chew slowly, and then to swallow slowly. It actually hurt going down, but soon a deliriously warm sensation spread from his abdomen outward. Just the one morsel had him feeling better than he had in two days.

Zach went on gnawing and eating, small sections at a time, relishing the meal as if it were his last. Which it might well be. There was no telling how long Kendrick would see fit to keep him alive. The man was as changeable as the wind, and might kill him whenever the whim struck.

As Zach ate, his arms were restored to normal. They tingled terribly for a long while, and when he eventually sought to bring them around in front of him, his sockets protested. It felt as if bone grated on bone. But he succeeded, and didn't move after that except to take more bites. He didn't want to draw attention to himself, didn't want his wrists tied again.

Ben Frazier finished and asked for another piece, but Vince Kendrick told him that was all they would get.

"Why waste more meat on you, old man, when after tomorrow your eating days will be over?"

That was when the trouble started. The Batson brothers, who had been keeping to themselves most of the day, stopped eating at the mention of what their leader had in store for the trapper. Billy said, "We've been meaning to talk to you about that, Mr. Kendrick."

"You don't say." The big man did not sound delighted at the news.

"My brother and I think it's wrong to murder Mr. Frazier. He never did us any harm. And he saved my brother's life."

Kendrick glanced at the older sibling. "This true, Frank? This how you feel?"

Frank Batson frowned. "Don' take that tone, Mr. Kendrick. We've stuck by you through thick and thin, haven't we? And we'll go on sticking by you. But yes, I feel we should let the old coot go once he's shown us where the gold is. It's the least we can do after what he did for me."

"Did you hear that, gents?" Kendrick said. "The farmers, here, think we're being too hard on gramps. Any of you agree?"

No one responded.

"Don't be shy," Kendrick declared. "I'd really like to know. I won't hold it against you. I won't be mad if you think you know better than me. I won't be offended if you believe I should step down and let someone else take over."

"Now, hold on, Mr. Kendrick," Billy said. "We never made any such claim."

Kendrick was a cauldron on the brink of boiling over. "Like hell you didn't! It's the same thing, no matter how you phrase it. You two think I'm making a bad decision. Which means I've got no business being the leader of this expedition. So go ahead. Take over, if either of you are man enough."

Frank Batson couldn't hide his worry. "Calm down, Mr. Kendrick. We have no hankering to be booshway. You're the boss. Not us. When we signed on, we agreed to always do as you say, remember?"

"Oh, I remember. The question is, do either of you? Apparently not, or you wouldn't be doubting me."

"All we're saying—" Frank began.

"Is that I don't know my ass from a prairie dog hole," Kendrick cut him off. "Well, think again. If we let the old buzzard live, he'll tell others what we did. Maybe you yokels don't care if a bunch of his friends track us down and fill us with lead, but I do."

Billy started to rise, but his brother gripped his shoulder. Tearing loose, the younger Batson snapped, "Of course we care. You're putting words in our mouths. And don't call us yokels. It's an insult."

"No fooling. But if it looks like a buffalo and smells like a buffalo and walks like a buffalo, odds are it's a buffalo."

"What do buffaloes have to do with anything?" Billy asked. Some of the men laughed, which added to his resentment. "That's enough! I'm sick and tired of being treated like a jackass. So help me, I'll shoot the next man who treats us like dirt." His hand wrapped around the butt of a pistol.

Silence descended. They all stopped eating. Ed Stark made as if to stand, but stayed where he was at a gesture from Vince Kendrick. Elden Johnson's arm drifted toward a rifle at his side.

"Sit down, little brother," Frank Batson said. "We don't want to get them mad at us. They don't mean anything by what they do."

"The hell they don't!"

"It's just their way of poking fun, is all," Frank said. "City folk do it all the time. You'll get used to it."

"Never," Billy said. "All my life I've had to put up with snotty people looking down their noses at me. I won't take it anymore. Just because I plow fields for a living doesn't make me dumb as an ox. I'm as smart as the next fellow."

"No one ever said you weren't." Frank tugged at his brother's shirt.

"Mr. Kendrick just did."

Vince Kendrick put down his meat. Wiping both

palms on his buckskins, he said quietly, "It's one thing to accuse me of not being fit to lead, another to threaten me. I want an apology, sonny."

"Don't call me that. I'm not your boy."

Like a rattler uncoiling, Kendrick slowly rose. "Say you're sorry, farmer. For your own sake."

"Say it," Frank urged.

"No," Billy answered.

"What can it hurt?" Cyrus Walton commented.

Elden Johnson's fingers were an inch from his Kentucky. "It's in your own best interests, youngster," he said.

Even Ira Sanders had an opinion. "If you have any brains, you'll do as Vince says."

"If I had any brains," Billy retorted, "I'd never have joined this trapping brigade. I should be home helping my ma and pa instead of wandering all over these mountains with the likes of you."

The potential for violence sizzled like frying bacon. Billy hadn't taken his hand off his flintlock, and Kendrick's fingers were close to one of his own. Another few moments and blood would be spilled. All of the men were as grim as a hangman. So the hearty laughter that pealed like a bell was all the more glaring.

Ben Frazier slapped his leg and rocked on his rump, exclaiming, "Yes! Yes! Go right ahead and shoot each other! It'll give the Utes that many less to kill. And give my friend and me a better chance to get away." He poked a bony finger at Billy. "Come on, boy! What are you waitin' for? Shoot that son of a bitch for treatin' you like a fool." Next he pointed at Kendrick. "And you! Show him he can't sass you and get away with it! Put one smack between his eyes!"

Ed Stark was fit to be tied. "Shut up, you damned loon!"

Zach smiled to himself. The ferret had it all backward. Frazier wasn't loony. He was canny as a fox, and was trying to save the younger Batson's life. Although why the trapper should go to the bother, Zach couldn't say.

Vince Kendrick was as incensed as Stark. "You'd like it if I killed this boy, wouldn't you, old man?"

"Hell, I'd like it better if both of you died," Frazier said gleefully. "Two less vermin in the world won't be missed."

For heartbeats the outcome hung in the balance. Then Kendrick hooked his thumbs in his belt and said, "Just to spite you, you old goat, I'm not going to do it. You'll have to try harder."

"Shucks," Frazier said.

Frank Batson nudged his brother. When Billy neither moved nor spoke, Frank nudged him harder and said, "Do it, damn you."

"I reckon I let my temper get the better of me, Mr. Kendrick. But I still think you treat us poorly at times."

Cyrus Walton snuffed out the last of Billy's anger by remarking, "Hell, kid. He doesn't treat you any different than he treats the rest of us. Vince was born cranky, and his disposition hasn't improved much over the years."

"Go to hell," Kendrick said.

Everyone laughed, including the Batson brothers. The crisis had passed. Frazier caught Zach staring at him and leaned close to whisper, "I know what you're thinkin'. I should've let them do it. But we need all these peckerwoods alive for when the Utes attack."

"What makes you so sure the Utes will?"

"Because they were followin' us for hours. You couldn't spot 'em, lyin' facedown over that horse like you were. But I did. And my guess is they're just waitin' for the right moment to catch us off guard." Frazier nodded at the men around the fire. "None of these greenhorns know it yet, but they're all dead men."

*   *   *

Louisa May Clark couldn't say what woke her. One moment she was adrift in dreamland—or, rather, a horrendous nightmare—and the next she was wide awake.

In her nocturnal flight of fear, Lou had been lost in an immense forest filled with gargantuan trees. For hours she wandered in a frantic effort to find a way out. But no matter which trail she took, they all brought her back to the same spot, to a small clearing in the center of the forest dominated by a bizarre marker, a chest-high pile of gleaming human skulls.

There were dozens of trails, but each and every one eventually led to the clearing and those terrible skulls.

All the while, Lou couldn't shake the feeling she was being stalked. That someone, or something, dogged her footsteps, always staying in the shadows so as not to be seen. Repeatedly she felt its baleful eyes on her back and whirled, and repeatedly there was nothing there.

Then Lou passed under a thick limb that hung low over her. As she did, the leaves rustled and a monstrous shadow engulfed her own. The thing had been lying in wait above. Startled, she threw back her head and clutched at a knife. But she was too slow. A shimmering sheet that resembled molten ink enfolded her within itself. She couldn't see, couldn't breathe. Desperate, she slashed and hacked, but the blade had no effect. Her lungs were close to bursting and she was close to dying when her eyes snapped open and she realized it had been a nightmare.

Lou couldn't shake the feeling of dread, however. Of evil menace and lurking terror. She saw that the fire had gone out, saw a multitude of stars testifying to the immensity of the firmament. About to try and go back to sleep, she experienced a shiver ripple down her spine when a soft rustling noise fell on her ears. The sound came from *behind* her. Just like in the nightmare. Only, this was real.

Lou still had her knife, but she had dropped the

pistol while she slept. Easing her hand to the ground, she groped for it. The rustling came a second time, louder, closer. An urge to flee almost overpowered her. Then her fingers closed on the smooth butt of her flintlock.

Something lightly brushed Lou's shoulder. It was all she could take. Spinning, she thrust with the knife. Only at the last possible moment did she check her thrust when she discovered who it was.

"Damn, sonny! You could kill a man like that!"

Bartholomew Dunne was on his side an arm's length away, propped on an elbow. He recoiled when the blade sought his throat.

"What do you think you're doing?" Lou demanded, sitting up.

"Trying to get to sleep. What does it look like?" In a huff, Dunne patted the blanket he had spread out. So near hers, the edges overlapped. "I just lay down and was going to wake you so you can keep watch."

Judging by the stars the night was half done. So Lou had no reason to distrust him other than her intuition. She was positive he had been about to do more than he said. But what? And why? "Fine, but next time don't lie so close. I don't like to be crowded."

"I'm sorry. I've forgotten how touchy whites can be."

Dunne's excuse rang hollow. Lou rose, wrapping her blanket over her shoulders. "Just so it doesn't happen again."

The crusty trapper curled up, pulled his own blanket to his chin, and was out to the world in under a minute, breathing deeply, sound asleep.

Lou had a nagging suspicion that he really wasn't, that he was peeking at her from under his eyelids. A silly notion, she told herself. But she couldn't shake it. She walked a dozen feet away and sat where he couldn't see her.

Yawning, Lou vigorously shook her head to help stay alert. Another ten or twelve hours of rest would suit her just fine. Her body felt as if it were made of marble, and her brain couldn't think fast enough to outrace a snail.

Lou thought of Stalking Coyote, of how he looked at her in their more private moments. Of the love he had shown, the tenderness, the concern. It comforted her. It filled her with a fuzzy feeling deep inside. Oh, what she wouldn't give to be able to take him into her arms and hug him silly! She prayed he was all right, and vowed that if any harm had come to him, she would see that the men responsible paid dearly.

Idly, Lou admired the heavenly spectacle, something she'd always liked to do when her pa was alive. Many a night, while he'd snored loud enough to rouse the dead, she had lain for hours staring at the stars and thinking.

On this night, Lou thought of a fascinating tidbit she had learned the summer before from a pilgrim bound for the Oregon Country. The man had claimed, incredibly, that Oberlin College was admitting women to its programs of higher learning, the first college in the country to do so.

Lou never had much schooling, and she was painfully conscious of the lack. At one point she'd had about made up her mind to go back to school once her pa and her returned to the States. After hearing about Oberlin, she'd even dreamed about going on to college, of becoming one of the first ladies in the country to have a degree.

Her father had thought it a crime against human nature. "Women need degrees like they need holes in their heads," he had complained. "Why, it's as bad an idea as giving women the right to vote."

But then, her pa was always railing against something or other. Lou harbored the idea he wasn't happy unless he was griping. She'd asked her ma about it once, and her mother had smiled in that knowing way of hers and said, "Some think the Almighty knew what He was doing when He made women and men so different. I say he used all the good ingredients making women and threw what was left into men.''

"But the Bible says God made Adam first," Lou had pointed out. "And that Eve was made from Adam's rib.''

"Then doctors and such have it all backwards. Our intelligence isn't in our heads. It's in our rib bones. And when the Good Lord took Adam's, He took what little intelligence Adam had.''

Lou had been shocked by her mother's blasphemous talk, yet she'd laughed heartily just the same. And it certainly did seem at times as if her pa were missing a few marbles. He was always chasing rainbows, always coming up with new schemes to get rich. Trapping had been his latest, and worst.

Lou never argued when he railed about higher learning. He could complain all he liked. She'd still planned to do as she darned well pleased.

Now her dream had been replaced by another.

Instead of seeking a degree, Lou was content to become Stalking Coyote's mate, to bear him children. To rear a family together. To spend the rest of their lives in close companionship.

It would be wonderful if Lou could somehow talk him into going back east so she could go to school, but she had to be realistic. The wilderness was Zach's home. He had lived in the mountains all his life. He despised most whites and wanted nothing to do with them. There was as much chance of him agreeing to live in the States as there was of the moon falling out of the sky and smashing to bits.

Lou could live with that, though. She'd rather have love than a piece of paper. A degree couldn't cherish her, couldn't keep her warm on a cold winter's night, couldn't make her laugh and feel giddy with delight at being alive. Stalking Coyote made her feel all those things, and so many more.

Sighing, Lou shifted position—and saw that Bartholomew Dunne had done the same. He was facing her again, and again she had the feeling he was watching her on the sly. Telling herself she was being foolish, that it was mere coincidence, Lou stood and walked past him to a flat boulder. Climbing up, she crossed her legs and roosted.

Another dream Lou had to abandon was her fond wish of one day seeing places like England and Europe. Her grandma was to blame. Seated at her grandmother's feet, Lou had listened to endless yarns about life in the Old Country. It had fired Lou's interest in other climes, other people.

Lou always wanted to visit Paris, in particular. Her grandma painted it as a worldly city, full of gaiety and charm. Many a time, Lou had imagined herself dressed in a fine flowing dress, sashaying along a crowded boulevard and drawing the eyes of all the handsome gentlemen she passed.

Making the trip would be easier than it had ever been. Steamships plied the Atlantic on regular runs now, their passengers enjoying all the comforts of home, and then some. Fine meals were served, and there was music and dancing.

A tinge of regret afflicted Lou. By taking Stalking Coyote as her husband, she was, in effect, putting an end to her two fondest dreams, attending college and venturing overseas. Hard sacrifices for anyone to make. *Is he worth it?* Lou asked herself, and promptly felt guilty for wondering such a thing.

Lou loved him. And love, true love, the kind of love that promised to last forever, was worth any sacrifice, great or small. Too many people went their whole lives being alone and lonely because they were unwilling to give up a few cherished notions for the greatest treasure any person could ever have.

Yes, Stalking Coyote was worth any cost. Lou would stick with him through thick and thin. She'd always be there when he needed her—as she was doing now by trying to save him. He would surely do the same for her.

Lou stifled another yawn. Lord, but she was tired. She scanned the area, grateful the night had grown quiet for a spell, and her gaze happened to alight on Bartholomew Dunne. He had turned once more and was facing her!

Resting a hand on a pistol, Lou slid off the boulder and walked toward him. Enough was enough. She would find out once and for all if he was awake or not.

Halfway there Lou heard his heavy breathing. She cat-footed nearer, and when she was an arm's length away he commenced to snore, as loudly as her father had done. It convinced her Dunne wasn't faking.

Lou felt silly. She was so overwrought about Stalking Coyote, she was imagining things. The trapper meant her no harm.

Relieved, Lou took to pacing. Adrift in thought, pondering the new life and new challenges that awaited her once she was wed, she lost all track of the passing minutes. So she was taken aback when a pink band framed the eastern horizon. Dawn wasn't far off. Soon they would be on their way, and she fully expected to be reunited with her beloved before the new day was done.

Lou got some coffee going. She saddled her horse and was set to go before the trapper stirred.

"Morning," Dunne greeted her. "You're a bundle of energy today."

"I'm looking forward to catching up with my friends."

"Let's hope we do. Then the whole bunch of us can head to Bent's Fort. From there, I'm off to the States. If you're smart, you'll do the same. After all, there's nothing here to hold you, is there?"

There was, but Lou wasn't about to tell him.

With the rising of the sun they were on the go again, Lou glued to the country ahead, hungry for her first glimpse of Stalking Coyote. She gave no thought to the man riding behind her.

Which was unfortunate. For, just as the day before, Bartholomew Dunne didn't take his eyes off her all morning.

Chapter Nine

Zachary King saw the first Ute shortly after the gold-hungry band of whites filed westward at the crack of dawn. Vince Kendrick was eager to reach Gold Mountain, and whenever the subject of the gold came up, his face glowed with the savage light of pure greed. The others were likewise infected now that they were close to their goal. Even the Batson brothers, who chatted amiably on about the kind of plow they should get for their father.

The whites were blinded by their lust. The gold was all they thought about, all they talked about. None stayed alert for hostiles except Elden Johnson, and more often than not he was distracted by the conversations of his companions.

Zach was always on the lookout. The meal and a night's sleep had refreshed him greatly. And he had something else to be thankful for. They hadn't tied him so he could ride sitting up, thanks largely to Kendrick's greed. The big man was so anxious to get to the gold that he had ordered Cyrus Walton to let Zach ride in order to make better time.

As they trotted toward a series of low hills, Zach spotted the first Ute. The warrior was hidden in pines to the southwest, observing them. No one else noticed. Zach glanced at Ben Frazier, who was fiddling with the whangs on his buckskins, and asked softly so only the trapper heard, "Do you see what I see?" He nodded at the hills.

Frazier spied the figure right away. Grinning, he said, "Well, lookee there. Told you, didn't I?"

"Why are you so happy?"

"Because I can't wait for the war party to make wolf meat of these bastards." Frazier glared at the head of the column. "Especially that polecat who pounded on me."

"The Utes will also kill us."

"Will they? I heard your pa was on good terms with them. Folks say he's the only white man they've let live in their territory. You're his son, so they're bound to spare you. And since I'm your friend, all you have to do is put in a good word and they'll spare me, too."

So that was it, Zach reflected. But the old-timer had misjudged badly. "My pa did the tribe a favor once, so they tolerate us. But there are a lot who would just as soon rub our family out."

"You're his son. That ought to count for something," Frazier insisted.

"It was my pa who did them the service, not me. Most of them have never even set eyes on me before. To those warriors out there, I'm just a half-breed. And part Shoshone, at that."

The trapper was beginning to worry. "The Shoshones are their enemies."

"Now you're catching on. I'm in as much danger as these whites. Maybe more, because any Ute warrior would be proud to have a Shoshone scalp hanging in his lodge."

"Damnation. I wish you'd mentioned this sooner. Our only hope, then, is to light a shuck when the gettin' is good."

That was their predicament in a nutshell, as the mountain men liked to say. Zach spent the morning on the watch for more painted figures but saw none until the sun was almost at its zenith. By then Gold Mountain loomed like a gigantic spike striving to impale the sky. Bleak and barren, it had an ominous air about it. Or so Zach thought.

The second Ute was on a hill to the north, in a stand of aspens, his buckskins and his dusky horse blending into the background so well that Zach wouldn't have spotted them if the horse hadn't twitched its tail.

What are the Utes waiting for? Zach asked himself. The war party should have struck the whites by this time. They outnumbered the whites two to one and had the element of surprise in their favor.

Maybe, Zach speculated, they had sent a rider for more warriors. Or perhaps—and this was more likely, in Zach's estimation—they were curious as to what the whites were up to. They were holding off until they learned what Kendrick's men were after. It couldn't be beaver, not in that area.

Ben Frazier was thinking along similar lines. Kneeing his mule up next to Zach's animal, he commented, "Why the deuce haven't those red rascals done anything yet? The Utes must be gettin' lazy. In the old days, they'd have swooped down on us the minute they saw us."

"Never look a gift horse in the mouth," Zach said.

"I'd rather they get it over with. If they kill me, so be it. I'll die content knowin' that Kendrick and his vultures have met their Maker, too. And when I run into 'em in Hell, I'll have the last laugh."

Elden Johnson picked that moment to holler, "Vince, we should give the horses a short rest. We've been pushing all morning."

It was plain Kendrick would rather keep going, but he called a halt. The water skin was passed around, and since there wasn't much water left, Zach and Frazier were denied a drink.

"Don't worry, my young friend," the trapper said. "We'll be at the stream in another couple of hours. We can drink our fill there."

"Provided they let us."

Soon the greed that goaded the whites showed itself again when Ed Stark remarked, "Vince, I've been thinking about the best way to divide up the gold. Each of us will get to take as much as we can carry, right?"

Kendrick was screening his eyes from the sun so he could study Gold Mountain. "Plus extra on the pack-horses and the old man's mule."

"That's what I thought," Stark said. "And we'll all get an equal share of what they carry. Which is only fair."

"Fairness be hanged. I'm booshway, aren't I? So I'm entitled to more. Most of the extra gold we pack out will belong to me."

The announcement met with universal disapproval. To a man, the whites frowned and exchanged looks critical of their leader.

Ed Stark opened his mouth, then hesitated. It was Cyrus Walton who voiced the sentiment on all their minds. "That doesn't hardly seem right, Vince. We share in the hardships but not the gold?"

"The captains of trapping brigades always get extra," Kendrick said. "That's how it's done and you know it."

"True," Cyrus Walton agreed. "But we're not a trapping brigade anymore, are we? We're after gold now, which means the rules don't apply."

Only then did Kendrick tear his gaze from the mountain. Only then did their expressions register. He reacted as he always did when someone opposed him: with rising anger. "Like hell they don't. Peltries, gold, it's all the same. I'm still the leader, I'm still entitled to more than the rest of you."

"Begging your pardon, Mr. Kendrick," Frank Batson said, "but there's a big difference between beaver hides and nuggets. I say we divide the gold fair and square so we all get the same amount.''

"I agree," Ira Sanders said.

"So do I," Elden Johnson declared.

Kendrick had an open rebellion on his hands. "You too, Elden?" he said in surprise. "After all we've been through, you'd side with them?"

"*Because* of all we've been through," the human anvil said. "Stark had it right for once. We should share and share alike."

"So that's how it is," Kendrick responded. "Even my best friends turn against me." Strangely enough, the big man's anger faded and he held up his hands in mock surrender. "I can see when I'm licked. If that's how you boys want it to be, that's how we'll do it. Once we reach St. Louis and convert the gold to money, we'll divide it up equally. Satisfied?"

The men greeted the announcement with smiles, but Zach was suspicious. Kendrick had given in much too easily. It wasn't like him to back down to their demands. The firebrand must have an ulterior motive, and Zach could guess what it was. Kendrick intended to see to it that no one else reached St. Louis alive. On the long trek across the prairie, they would all suffer fatal mishaps or mysteriously disappear. Kendrick was in the unbreakable grip of gold madness; he wanted it all for himself.

"Sounds good to me, Vince," Cyrus Walton said.

"I can't hardly wait" was how Ed Stark felt.

"Won't Pa be tickled?" Billy Batson asked his older brother. "He thought this whole trapping business was a waste of time. That nothing good would come of it. But we'll show him."

"That we will," Frank concurred.

Of them all, only Elden Johnson wasn't pleased. His forehead was furrowed, and he regarded Kendrick as he might a pet wolf that had turned on him. Johnson was the one person Kendrick hadn't fooled.

Presently, in high spirits, they traveled on. Within

an hour they neared the base of Gold Mountain. Their excitement grew and grew, to where several constantly fidgeted in their saddles as if they had ants in their britches. Hopeful faces were craned upward, the gleams in their eyes blinding them to the peril they were in.

Vince Kendrick reined up and beckoned to Frazier. No one objected when Zach tagged along to hear what was said.

"We're here, old man. So tell me where the gold is. And if you've been lying to us, you'll suffer worse than if Comanches got their hands on you. I guarantee it."

"Unlike some folks I could name, I'm partial to always tellin' the truth." Frazier pointed at a high slope, at a stream glittering in the sunlight like a diamond necklace. "It's up there, but I have to show you exactly where."

"How long will it take?"

"Not much over two hours, I should reckon."

It took closer to three, but no one seemed to mind once they came to the stream, which flowed diagonally down across the mountain and on into lush woodland far below. Walton and Sanders crossed to the other bank. As excited as school kids on a picnic, the whole band climbed higher, each trying to be the first to spot nuggets.

Frazier found their antics humorous. "Look all you want," he told them, "but the gold is only along one short stretch."

The going became rough and steep. Zach checked their back trail frequently but saw no evidence of Utes. They were there, though. He was sure of it.

Along about four in the afternoon, the old trapper crested a rise and drew rein on an upland bench dotted with firs and sprinkled with boulders. The gurgling stream divided it into two sections. Random pools were separated by rapids, but nowhere was the water more than a couple of feet deep.

"Why did you stop?" Vince Kendrick demanded.

"This is it," Frazier said.

"What?"

Frazier laughed. "What else? Yonder is where I made my strike."

Ed Stark whooped and spurred his mount down to the water's edge. He was out of the saddle and in the stream before the animal came to a halt. Bending, he started moving stones on the bottom and prying at rocks along the bank. Suddenly his hand dipped. "I found one!" he exclaimed. "Look here! Honest-to-God gold, boys!"

Yipping and chortling, the rest barreled down to join him. Kendrick, Walton, Sanders, Johnson, they were all swept by gold fever. Fanning out, they plunged in, scouring the bed for more precious ore.

"Look at 'em," Frazier said to Zach. "Dumber than stumps, the whole lot." He winked. "What they don't know is that I cleaned out most of the gold. Have it cached close by where no one but me will ever find it."

Sanders was crowing and flapping his arms like a rooster gone berserk. He had found a nugget, too, and was beside himself with joy.

"Oh, there's some left," Frazier said, "but mostly smaller nuggets I didn't bother with. I bet if I took the time to pan, I'd probably find a ton more. And that doesn't count the grains that must be mixed with the gravel and dirt at the bottom."

Now it was Billy Batson who squealed and held aloft a prize.

Zach saw that all the whites practically had their noses in the water. "This is our chance," he said, and reined his horse around. No one looked up, no one cried out. His captors had one thing on their mind, and one thing alone.

Zach went over the rise at a brisk walk. An incline linked the bench to a lower slope, and he had to be careful his mount didn't lose its footing. Any faster and they courted disaster.

The trapper was close behind, grinning fiercely. "Those idiots! We'll be long gone before they notice we've cut out on them."

But Frazier was mistaken. Zach was only halfway down the incline when someone—Elden Johnson?— let out with a shout loud enough to be heard in the States.

"The breed and the old coot are getting away!"

By midday Louisa was tired and hungry and thirsty, but she didn't care. She would ride all day and all night if that was what it took to catch up with Stalking Coyote. Twice she had paid no heed to suggestions by Bartholomew Dunne that they stop and rest, but now she had to. The dun was caked with sweat, and Dunne's pack animal was flagging.

Tall pines hemmed them in. For quite some time they had been traveling through shadowed, murky forest, the gloom adding to Lou's depression. She yearned for open country, for sunshine, for the sight of distant horsemen.

"Didn't you hear me?" Dunne asked when she didn't respond right away. "My horse is tuckered out. Let's give the animals a breather."

Lou's heart waged war with her better judgment, and her better judgment won. Barely. Sliding down, she wrapped the reins around a bush. "How far ahead of us do you think they are?"

Dunne squatted and examined the tracks. "I'd say three or four hours, not much more. They haven't stopped once, and that puzzles me. Why are they in such a consarn hurry?"

"I don't rightly know."

"Greeners are always a mite peculiar." Dunne gazed at her. "Always putting on airs, acting as if they know all there is to know about living in the wilds, when they don't know a bear's hind end from their own.''

Lou turned her back to him. Greenhorns weren't the only ones who acted high and mighty. Dunne had a knack for it himself.

"Take your friends, for instance. They left their homes and kin to become trappers. They rode pretty near a thousand miles, came all this way, for nothing. If they had taken the time to ask around before they left, they'd have spared themselves a lot of aggravation.''

"How was anyone to know? We thought beaver fur was as popular as ever." Lou was tired of her charade, but she couldn't have him divining the truth.

"One of the first lessons I ever learned was to always look before I leap." Dunne slowly approached. "Another was to never judge others by how they appear. Appearances can be tricky.''

"That they can," Lou absently agreed, not interested one whit in what he had to say.

"Take you, for instance.''

"Me?''

"No one would ever guess the truth.''

Louisa pivoted. She didn't like how he was staring at her, didn't like the budding leer on his face. "What truth?''

"Did you think I wouldn't catch on?''

"I have no idea what you're taking about," Lou bluffed.

"You're a liar," Bartholomew Dunne stated flatly. Stopping, he cradled his rifle in the crook of an elbow. "I've got to admit, you had me fooled for quite a while. You look like a boy and dress like a boy, but under those buckskins is something else entirely.''

"What do you mean?" Lou asked, a terrible premonition stealing over her, to be dwarfed by surging rage.

"I had to find out. Last night while you were asleep,

I checked. I touched you. Only once, mind, but it was enough to—''

Lou flew at him, hitting his chin, his chest. But he was much larger, much heavier. Her blows had no telling effect. Stepping back, she grabbed for a flint-lock. Dunne was on her in a quick stride, the stock of his rifle sweeping out and in. It drove into the pit of her stomach, doubling her over.

''We can't have you shooting me,'' the trapper mocked.

A foot lashed out, snagging Lou's ankle. She was shoved onto her back and a moccasin was placed on her chest.

''Behave and it'll go easier.''

Lou punched his leg. Without warning, Dunne stomped on her. It felt as if her ribs caved in, and for terrible moments she couldn't catch her breath. Blurred vision prevented her from interfering as Dunne stripped her of weapons.

''You won't be needing these, girly. Now, why don't you tell me who you really are and what you're really doing here.''

Mad enough to rip into him tooth and nail, Lou marshaled her strength and did just that. But as she surged up off the ground, his rifle surged down and clipped her on the temple. She sprawled on her belly, her ears ringing, bright dots floating before her eyes.

''I can wallop you until the cows come home,'' Dunne said. ''Or you can spare yourself a mountain of misery by answering me.'' He placed a foot on her neck and pressed. ''What's your real name?''

Anguish speared Lou like a Sioux lance. ''I've already told you. Lou Clark.''

''The truth, girl.'' Dunne ground his heel down.

''Louisa May Clark!'' she shouted, thrashing.

''Louisa? Ah. That's better. And how old are you?''

Lou was about to lie, to claim she was older than she actually was, but a tiny voice warned her to do the opposite. ''I'm fourteen.''

"That young?" Dunne removed his foot and stepped back. "I took you for slightly older. Why, you must be pure as the driven snow."

"So?"

"So it complicates things."

"I don't understand."

"You will, girly. You will."

Lou didn't like the sound of that. Frustration, outrage, and yes, fear, threatened to sap her will, to turn her to mush, but she resisted, rallied, and sat up.

"Who are we chasing?" Dunne inquired. "The truth," he warned. "Don't insult me by saying it's a brigade of free trappers. I've had doubts all along."

"It's my family and some friends." Lou fabricated more falsehoods in the hope it would influence how he treated her. "My ma, my pa, my brothers and others. Harm me and they'll make you pay."

Dunne clucked like an irate hen. "You don't know when to stop, do you?" His foot was a blur. It caught her on the shoulder and dumped her onto her back. "If they were kin of yours, they'd be scouring these mountains from top to bottom. But they're only interested in getting somewhere fast. Hell, they don't even know you exist, do they?"

"One is a friend of mine," Louisa hedged, pushing up again. Her shoulder was sore but otherwise fine. "Honest."

"And the rest? Do they know about you?"

Lou was set to say yes, but Dunne anticipated her and balled his left fist. "No. Except for my friend." Inspiration prompted her to add, "They took her against her will."

"Her? It's another girl?"

"No, she's older than me. A grown woman. Twenty-four. And a lot lovelier than I'll ever be."

Dunne was intently interested. "You don't say? And you have no idea who these jaspers are?"

"I never saw them before. They stole into camp while I was off gathering wood, bundled her onto a horse, and lit out. I've been after them ever since.''

"What were the two of you doing all alone?"

"We were on our way back from Bent's Fort. My folks settled in a valley northeast of here about a year and a half ago. Her family showed up eight or nine months later. We've been best friends ever since.''

"More stinking settlers?" Bartholomew Dunne scratched his lice-ridden beard. "They're multiplying like rabbits. Must be fifteen to twenty by now. Next thing you know, they'll build a town, and the mountains will never be the same.''

A hundred towns could spring up, for all Louisa cared. She measured the distance between them, calculating whether she could wrest a pistol from him before he knocked her down again, or worse. "You believe me, then?''

Dunne guffawed good-naturedly. "Girly, something tells me you're the god-awfullest liar who ever lived. I'll believe every word you say the day cows learn to fly. But I'll give you the benefit of the doubt for now.''

"Thank you.''

"For what? I'm not doing it out of the kindness of my heart. If you weren't so scrawny, I'd make do with you.''

The insult incited Lou to snap, "Scrawny, am I? I'll have you know a certain fella thinks I'm as pretty as a peach.''

"He must need spectacles. I've seen chickens with more meat on their bones than you.''

His comments left Lou momentarily speechless. Sputtering, she stammered, "Why—why—you're the most insulting man I've ever met! Have you no shame?''

"Not a lick,'' Dunne unabashedly admitted while sidestepping to his packhorse. From a parfleche he removed a coiled rope.

"What's that for?''

"A smart girl like you should be able to figure it out.'' Dunne leveled his rifle, then tossed the rope at her. "Make a loop over your wrists. I'll do the rest."

"I'd rather be shot."

"Would you indeed?" The trapper thumbed back the hammer. "Riling me wouldn't be smart. It's been a hellacious long time since I've had a white gal, and I have a powerful hankering. Scrawny as you are, you're still a female." He paused. "But I'd much rather treat myself to a full-grown woman. This friend of yours, what's her name?"

Lies now came as smoothly as melted butter to Lou's tongue. "Zelda. Short for Griselda."

"What's she look like?"

"She's about your height, with long blond hair and blue eyes and—"

Bartholomew Dunne jerked as if slapped. "A blonde! That's too good to be true. I've always had a fondness for yellow hair. The way it sparkles like gold! I love to run my fingers through it."

Lou remembered her mother lecturing her on men like Dunne. Men whose main interest in life was what went on behind locked doors with the curtains drawn. There were words for men like him, but Lou was too much the lady to even think them.

"She'd better be as good-looking as you say," Dunne said. "After getting my hopes up, I won't take kindly to being made a fool of." He hefted the rifle. "Now, make that loop. I want to take a gander at your friend."

Lou did as she was instructed. For now, she must obey. But she had better come up with a scheme to gain the upper hand, or when they caught up with the cutthroats Dunne was liable to punish her by doing things no man had ever done, and no one but Zach ever should. Three or four hours was all she had.

Would it be enough?

Chapter Ten

Zachary King sorely wished he were on his dun. It was exceptionally surefooted, had tremendous stamina, and responded to the lightest touch on the reins. The animal he was now riding stumbled going down the incline, nearly pitching him off. Whether it possessed much stamina remained to be seen. As for responding to the reins, it was one of those horses that fought the bit and resented being controlled. He had to haul on the reins with all his might to get it to veer to the left so when they reached the bottom they would be near some pines.

Any cover was preferable to none. Zach felt exposed on the incline, his shoulder blades prickling in anticipation of taking a slug in the back. Judging from the shouts and curses rising from the bench, Kendrick's men were scrambling to their mounts and would soon be in frenzied pursuit.

Zach glanced back to see how Frazier was faring. The trapper wore a wide grin, as if he were enjoying himself immensely. His mule kept up with the horse with no problem, moving as surefootedly as the dun would.

"Go, Bessy! Go!" the old-timer hollered.

They were almost to a shelf that crowned the next slope when a roar of rage brought Zach's head around. Vince Kendrick was at the rim and was raising his rifle.

Kendrick didn't command them to stop. He didn't warn them that he was going to shoot. He simply wedged the stock to his shoulder, fixed a hasty bead, and fired.

Zach was the intended target. He bent low as the rifle spewed smoke and heard the lead whiz above him.

More greenhorns appeared. By then Zach was on the shelf and among the pines. Frazier was right behind him, cackling merrily. Being shot at amused him even more.

It didn't amuse Zach. Racing to the slope, he descended at a breakneck clip. The ground wasn't quite as steep, and he could go faster but still not fast enough to suit him. Kendrick and three or four others were hurtling downward, well within rifle range.

Dense forest offered the safest haven, but the nearest heavy growth was a mile away, to the southwest. On Gold Mountain itself vegetation was sparse. Unnaturally so, in Zach's opinion, since all the other mountains in that region were covered with lush woods. Why Gold Mountain should be different was a mystery. Maybe there was something in the soil. Or maybe, as the Shoshones would say, Gold Mountain was bad medicine.

The Shoshones believed there were bad places, evil places, places that should be shunned. They never went near certain lakes, valleys, and mountains because legend had it anyone who did died. When Zach was younger, he'd thought it silly of them. Until one day his pa told him every legend had a basis in fact, and he should heed the wisdom of the ancients.

A friend of his pa's named Scott Kendall had related a story that shed light on his pa's outlook. It seemed that years ago Zach's father and some others had boldly ventured into a valley believed by all the tribes, not just the Shoshones, to be a place best shunned.

Zach's pa would never talk about what happened there, except to say that Zach must never, ever visit the valley.

Then along came Scott Kendall, who knew the particulars and had shared them with Zach. It was a harrowing tale of giant hairy creatures that devoured human flesh, of rank-smelling beasts who slaughtered red and white men alike with chilling abandon.

One day Zach would like to go to that valley and see the creatures for himself.

The blast of a rifle and the sizzle of hot lead shattered Zach's remembrance. He scolded himself for letting his attention lapse, a mistake unworthy of a Shoshone warrior. Concentrating on riding to the best of his ability, he flew past scrub brush, the hooves of his mount spraying dirt and dust.

Ben Frazier whooped with delight.

All the whites were after them now, the Batson brothers straggling well behind the rest. Elden Johnson had caught up with Kendrick and kept trying to steady his rifle, but the bobbing and lurching of his mount hampered him. That didn't stop Ira Sanders from firing, though. The shot went wild, and Ben Frazier cackled louder than ever.

For over half a mile the chase continued, before tragedy struck.

Zach could see the base of Gold Mountain. The edge of the forest was so close yet so far. Skirting a boulder, he lashed his horse. Higher up another rifle cracked. A high-pitched squeal rent the air, then a horrified outcry. There was a tremendous crash. Looking back, Zach was dismayed at the sight of the trapper's mule sliding on its side amid a shower of dust and stones, with Frazier clinging in desperation to the saddle.

Tugging on the reins, Zach brought his animal to a stiff-legged stop. He wheeled and hurried to his friend's side. The mule was shaking and heaving, blood spouting from its nostrils and mouth. A ball had caught it high in the side—puncturing a lung, from the look of things. It wouldn't last long.

Frazier clung to its neck, wailing like a child, near hysterical in his grief. "No, Bessy! Please, God! No! No! No!"

Zach bent and extended his bound wrists. "Quickly! Swing up behind me!"

The trapper didn't budge. Tears streaking his grizzled cheeks, Frazier stroked the mule and blubbered, "Don't die, old girl! Please don't die! I'll fix you up and you'll be back on your feet in no time! You'll see!"

What Zach saw were seven angry men bearing down on them. Smoke curled from the barrel of Elden Johnson's rifle; he was the one who had brought Bessy low. "Hurry, Ben!" Zach urged. "Climb on before it's too late!"

Frazier waved him off. "Go! Light a shuck! I won't abandon her, not while she's still alive. Save yourself if you can."

"*Please!*" Zach pleaded, in vain.

"Oh, my sweet, sweet Bessy," the trapper said, crying unashamedly. "Without you I don't know what I'll do."

Cold laughter from on high gave Zach an idea. "Do you hear that, Ben? They're poking fun at you. They shot your mule just to catch us. They've won, because you won't leave her and I won't leave you."

Sniffling, Frazier glared at the greenhorns. "You sons of bitches! You've killed the kindest critter any man ever owned! She has a heart of gold, this old girl."

Bessy stopped quivering. Her tongue had protruded,

and her eyes were as blank as shale. Zach bent lower to snatch at the trapper's shirt. "She's gone, Ben. You can't avenge her if Kendrick catches us. I'm begging you. Climb up while we still have a chance to get away. Another minute and it will be too late."

Frazier lowered his lips to the mule's neck and tenderly kissed her. "Good-bye, Bess. I'll miss you more than you'll ever know. And I'll make the varmints who did this pay." Rising unsteadily, he wrapped his fingers around Zach's arms, then nodded. "Pull me up."

Another shot boomed, courtesy of Cyrus Walton. The clerk aimed too low, and the slug meant for them thudded into Bessy instead.

"I've never hated anyone in all my born days as much as I hate those butchers!" Frazier declared.

Zach didn't reply. He had to devote all his energy to reaching the forest. The horse balked at bearing an extra burden, but once Zach slapped his heels and flicked the reins, it broke into a gallop.

Frazier was shaking a fist at their pursuers. "Filthy murderers! If it's the last thing I ever do, I'll see that you're wiped out to the last man!"

Zach wished the trapper would sit still. The lower slopes were split by gullies and ravines he must avoid, as well as treacherous talus. He spied a rattlesnake sunning itself and immediately slanted to the left so the horse wouldn't see it.

A rifle banged, then a second, and a third. Leaden hornets scorched the air on all sides. Zach twisted and saw that Kendrick and company had halted and jumped off their mounts. They were firing and reloading as swiftly as they could, volley after volley, in an all-out attempt to bring the horse down before it was out of range.

Ben Frazier was cussing up a storm, heaping every vile word in the English vocabulary on Bessy's slayers.

Zach started to believe they would make it. Another

hundred yards and they would be too far off for even the most skilled marksman in the world to hit. Suddenly, large boulders barred his path and he had to swing to the right to go around. For nerve-racking moments they were broadside to their enemies, the horse as inviting a target as anyone could ask for. Slugs peppered the boulders and stitched the soil, spewing miniature geysers.

Frazier went on railing like a madman, his voice growing hoarse. Suddenly he fell silent and slumped to one side.

"Ben?"

The old man uttered a groan in Zach's ear, clutched at his arm, and fell. Zach reached around, but his hand closed on empty air. Reining up, horror filled him. Frazier lay still, a scarlet stain on the front of his shirt.

"Ben!"

Zach vaulted off, holding on to the reins to keep the horse from bolting. Up above, Kendrick's men were reloading for another volley. Zach sprang to the trapper, whose eyes were closed, and grasped his hand. "Can you hear me, Ben? We have to get out of here!" But his companion lay as limp as a wet cloth. Zach hastily felt for a pulse and couldn't find one.

Spinning, Zach swore at the culprits as lustily as the trapper had done. Some laughed, and Cyrus Walton clapped Elden Johnson on the back as if congratulating him.

"Damn you!" Zach cried in impotent fury, then swung onto the horse. Johnson was taking aim again. As Zach hurtled into motion, Johnson's rifle spat death. But the ball whistled by and ricocheted off one of the boulders. Loping past them, Zach made for the trees with renewed fervor.

Kendrick was thundering at his band to mount up and give chase. They weren't about to give up, even if it delayed their search for the gold.

Which suited Zach just fine.

*   *   *

The mountain man came to the top of the bluff and lingered just long enough to read the sign. On a tether was the mare. Strapped to the empty saddle were two rifles, both Hawkens, guns he was as familiar with as he was his own.

The bearded seeker had backtracked the mare's flight into the woods, finding the long guns and her along the way. The horse had not run off, had, in fact, been glad to see him. And why shouldn't she, when he had raised her from a foal?

The tracks had shown him where a great bear stalked the girl, and he had deduced how close she came to having her flesh shredded to ribbons. He could well imagine the fright she must have felt, and his heart went out to her.

He was becoming anxious for her safety, and his son's. Being sidetracked had proven a costly delay. He mustn't waste another minute. Until they were found, he wouldn't sleep, wouldn't eat. By switching from his bay to the mare when one tired, he could maintain a steady pace for hours on end.

His green eyes hardened at the thought that harm might have befallen those he sought. If so, whoever was to blame would rue the day they came into the world. He wasn't a violent man by nature. But decades of wilderness life had imbued him with the ferocity of the beasts he shared the wilderness with. When he had to, he could kill, and could do so with skill that surpassed the ability of most.

The big man hoped his worry was unwarranted. He prayed the boy and girl were well. At moments like this, he almost regretted the decision he had made long ago to stay in the mountains rather than return to civilization. Almost, but not quite. Sure, Nature was a cruel mistress. Sure, surviving in the Rockies was a formidable challenge. And sure, of the hundreds of hopefuls who had flocked to the mountains to reap their fortunes in the beaver trade, only a handful were still breathing. But the benefits far outweighed the risks.

Where else could a man live as free as the birds? Where else could a person do as they pleased, when they pleased, without being beholden to anyone? Without having politicians hold sway over all aspects of his life? Without being hamstrung by confining laws that turned freedom into thinly disguised slavery?

To the mountain man, the Rockies were literally heaven on earth. He had taken to them like a duck to water. To the thrill of being the master of his own destiny. To the excitement of living each day to the full instead of toiling day in and day out at a boring job.

Life was meant for living. Humankind was meant to be free. Maybe the legions who dwelled in squalid hovels in cramped cities lorded over by the well-to-do were willing to accept their plight, but not him. He refused to go through life burdened by chains devised by those who had no right to impose their edicts on anyone.

The cost of true freedom was constant vigilance. He had heard that somewhere, and it was true. But it seemed to him that most people no longer rated freedom worth the price. They were all too ready to have others run their lives. So long as they were well-fed and clothed and had a roof over their heads, they were content.

Therein lay the greatest danger. Contentment bred laziness. People became so accustomed to being led on a leash and having their needs met by others that they forgot how to fend for themselves.

The big man smiled grimly. That would never happen to him. He would go to his grave as proud and free as the bald eagle soaring high overhead.

It was a source of no small pride to him that he had been able to bestow the same precious gift on his son. And he would destroy, without qualms, anyone and everyone who tried to deprive any member of his family of their birthright.

Louisa May Clark was conscious of every passing second. Two hours had gone by. Two hours! And she had yet to think of a means to escape from Bartholomew Dunne. Her wrists were bound in front of her so she couldn't work at them without Dunne noticing. He was leading her horse and the pack animal, both, and whistling cheerfully as he had been doing for quite some time. "Don't your lips ever get tired?" she asked.

"Is that your way of saying I'm grating on your nerves?" Dunne laughed. "Be nice, girly. It helps me pass the time. You can join in if you're of a mind."

"I'd rather eat rocks."

Glancing at her, Dunne smirked. "Sassy little filly, aren't you? Maybe I should tell you a story."

"It wouldn't interest me."

"Some years back I met a trader who makes trips to Santa Fe now and then. He had heard about this white gal who was taken by the Indians. The Apaches or some such. She had a lot of sand, that gal, but she was also the worst shrew who ever lived. She'd tongue-lash a parson for misquoting Scripture."

"She doesn't sound at all like me," Lou said.

"I'm not done. You see, a warrior took this gal for his own. And all she did was gripe. Gripe, gripe, gripe. Nothing suited her. Not the food, not the clothes they made her wear. One day she complained that he was working her too hard, so he put an end to her shrewish ways once and for all."

"How?" Lou asked, despite herself.

"He cut out her tongue."

"You made that up to scare me."

"That's not all. He let it dry, tied it to a rawhide cord, and hung it around her neck. She had to wear it as a constant reminder of what wagging her tongue had cost."

"Are you fixing to cut out my tongue if I don't shut up?"

"The notion did occur to me."

"You like to hurt women, don't you?"

Dunne reined up so abruptly, Lou's horse nearly walked into his mount. His hand dropped to his Green River knife. "Prod too hard and you won't like the result. You need to learn to keep your rightful place, girly, and I'm just the one to teach you."

"My rightful place?" Lou quizzed him.

"Haven't you heard? In the greater scheme of things, women are inferior to men. Females aren't as strong, aren't as smart. So us men have the natural right to lord it over you women as we see fit."

"That's the silliest idea I've ever heard."

"Believe me, this world would be much better off if women would just do as they're told. Men are born leaders. We were created to run things. Government, businesses, the family, you name it." Dunne swatted at a fly. "I learned it from my pa. He used to beat my ma whenever she got too uppity, but she doted on him hand and foot."

Louisa was astounded. She couldn't believe how wrong she had been about him. Dunne was about as kindly as a wolverine.

"Women were put on this earth to satisfy male needs. Your sole purpose in life is to make us happy. To do whatever we see fit, no questions asked."

"You're crazy."

"There are lots of men who feel the way I do, girly. Most are too weak-kneed to admit it, though. And I can't blame them none. Back in the States it could get a fella into a lot of trouble." Dunne encompassed the mountains with a grand motion. "It's part of the reason I came west. Partly why I took up trapping as my trade."

Lou couldn't say what made her utter her next comment. A hunch, maybe. Her ma always said women were more sensitive to the thoughts and feelings of others. "You're the one who got into trouble, aren't you? What did you do? Hurt someone? Do you beat women like your pa did?"

Bartholomew Dunne reined up again, and sighed. "That's another thing. Women are always trying to get our goat. Your kind just aren't happy unless they're making us miserable."

"You're avoiding the question," Lou said, and the trapper stared at her so long and so menacingly that she braced for a slap or a punch.

"Think you know it all? Yes, I got into a little scrape. I busted a woman's jaw. She and I were to be hitched. Then the bitch up and changed her mind with only a couple of months to go until our wedding. So I beat on her a little."

"A little?"

"Her folks filed a complaint against me. Wanted to charge me with murder. I cut out and haven't been back since."

To look at him, Lou would never suspect he was a heartless brute. He seemed so *ordinary*. He didn't foam at the mouth or gnaw on trees or do any of the other things rabid animals did, but he was just as mad as any wolf afflicted with the disease. And she was completely at his mercy.

"Why are you staring at me like that?"

"No special reason," Lou fibbed, averting her face.

In a huff, Dunne yanked on the lead ropes. She watched him out of the corner of an eye, biding her time as he sulked for a spell. Gradually, his moodiness faded and he relaxed. When he commenced to whistle again, she shifted and gripped the pommel.

Lou wasn't going to wait any longer. It wouldn't make a difference when she tried to get away. One time was as good as another, so she might as well do it now. They were in heavy woodland, with plenty of cover. The key was to separate Dunne from his rifle, and his horse, long enough for her to reach it.

Through a gap in the canopy a mountain appeared.

Zach's abductors were making straight for it. She was at a loss to explain why. The country was new to her. All she knew was that the Utes claimed it as their own, and woe to anyone who disputed them.

"Bartholomew," she said sweetly, "mind if I ask a question?"

"Not when you ask like that. What is it?"

"How well do you know this area?"

"As well as any mountaineer, I expect. There were never many beaver to speak of, and water is scarce, so most fought shy of it. I only pass through now and then on my way to Bent's Fort."

Lou had him snared, but he didn't realize it. He had completely let down his guard. "Ever seen any Utes other than those you saw yesterday?"

Dunne swiveled. "Hereabouts? No, but I've seen a lot of sign. Why?"

"I was just wondering if they always mark trees like that one there," Lou said, pointing ahead and to the left.

"Trees?" The trapper gazed in the direction she indicated. "What are you dithering about? I don't see any marks—"

It was all the further he got. Lou slammed her heels against her mount the instant Dunne turned and Stalking Coyote's horse shot forward like a bolt of lightning. She was next to Dunne in a twinkling, her foot rising and ramming into his ribs as he began to swing toward her. Lou threw all her weight and power into the kick in an effort to unseat him, but she wasn't entirely successful.

Bartholomew squawked as he toppled. Flailing wildly, he would have fallen if his right foot hadn't snagged in the stirrup. As it was, he hung half on, half off, unable to right himself—and unable to use his rifle.

Lou sped into the trees, gaining speed rapidly. The dun was a marvel, the best horse she'd ever handled. She threaded among the trunks with a precision she

141

never believed she was capable of, and she owed most of it to the horse. The trapper's curses blistered her ears, making her giggle. *She had shown him!*

Or had she? Lou covered forty more feet and was giving a broad pine a wide berth when the sharp retort of the trapper's Kentucky warned her he was back in the saddle. The ball struck the pine with a loud thump. In seconds she was beyond it and temporarily out of Dunne's sight.

As Lou rode, she gnawed at the rope on her wrists. It was thick and grimy and tasted awful, but she severed strand after strand and had chewed a quarter of the way through when a low limb forced her to stop and dip over the dun's side to avoid being torn off its back. Simultaneously, a rifle boomed, and the slug that would have cored her skull buzzed harmlessly above her.

Wrath rode Bartholomew Dunne's brow, even as he rode his horse, guiding it by his legs alone, and began to reload.

To the right was a thicket. Ordinarily, Lou wouldn't think of entering one on horseback. The small limbs and sharp points inflicted considerable pain. But extreme situations called for extreme measures. She reined the dun on in, wincing at a pang in her ankle.

The trapper scorched the heavens with a new litany of foul oaths. Lowering his ramrod, he slowed, then angled to the west to go around.

Lou quickly reined to the east. Barbs tore at the dun's chest and legs, but the dependable animal never broke stride. It nickered when a limb gashed it low on the shoulder, and again when its cheek was lanced. The racket they made was enough to bring the entire Ute nation on the run, and Lou could only hope that Bartholomew Dunne didn't realize she had changed direction.

The end of the thicket materialized.

Lou smiled and patted the dun as they broke into the open. Already she was thinking of how she would circle in a wide loop and take up the trail of the men who had abducted Stalking Coyote. Belatedly, it hit her that she would be better off searching for sign of her own abductor. Just then she swept past a wide trunk, and the stock of a rifle blossomed before her eyes. Lou brought up her arms to protect herself, but the blow still lifted her clear off her mount and toppled her head over heels into high weeds.

Dazed, her mind reeling, Lou struggled to rise. A moment later a blurry shape towered over her and she was brutally knocked onto her back.

"You shouldn't have done that, girly. You really shouldn't. Now I reckon that blonde will have to wait. I'm about to make a woman of you."

Chapter Eleven

Killing and slaughter had been part and parcel of Zachary King's life since he was old enough to remember. One of his earliest memories was of standing beside the bodies of four Utes his father had slain. This was before the truce, before the tribe granted permission for the Kings to live in Ute country, back in the days when the tribe was doing all it could to drive his father out. Zach vividly recalled the pulsing blood, the pungent scent of it, the slick feel of it on his palm when he touched one of the warriors before his mother could stop him.

For the Shoshones, warfare was woven into the fabric of their lives. The men lived to count coup, to gain honor in battle. Zach could recollect sitting in a lodge on his father's lap, many a night, listening to prominent warriors talk about the great fights they had taken part in. He'd heard them describe in gory detail how they slew enemies. And, in his childish way, he had feasted on the slaughter like a young wolverine.

Zach, himself, had killed before. Not a lot of times.

Not as often as he would have liked. But enough that he could do so when it was necessary with no hesitation whatsoever, and no regrets afterward. His life had taught him that to kill others was normal, something that simply had to be done now and then. Remorse was an alien concept. Why be upset over killing someone who had been trying to kill him?

Zach had been at a rendezvous some years back when a minister showed up, a godly man bound for the Oregon Country with his wife. The pair told Zach's mother that the Lord had anointed them to convert heathens to the one true God. Zach had been intrigued by the man's talk of love and brotherhood until the subject of the Ten Commandments came up. When he heard the minister read from the Bible, "Thou shalt not kill," Zach had lost all interest and wandered off. Any religion so silly was not worth his time.

Had Zach done as the Bible commanded, he'd have died long ago. The Blackfeet, the Bloods, the Comanches and Apaches, they had never heard of "turning the other cheek" or "doing unto others as you would have them do unto you." They would laugh at such notions. To them, as to the Shoshones, an enemy was someone who *must* be slain. It was kill or be killed. Or, more appropriately, kill *first* or be killed.

Now, as Zach raced toward the forest with seven gold-crazed whites in grim pursuit, all he thought about was killing them. Killing each and every one, in horrible and bloody ways. They were enemies, and enemies must be destroyed.

For slaying his friend they had earned Zach's undying hatred. Ben Frazier had been one of the few decent whites Zach knew, one of the few who didn't despise him for being a half-breed. Frazier had never looked down his nose at Zach, as so many whites did. Ben Frazier accepted Zach as just another person, and for that he would always be grateful.

Suddenly a rifle cracked. Invisible fingers plucked

at the whangs on Zach's right arm, but he was spared from harm. He looked back. It had been Elden Johnson again, the best shot in the brigade, the most dangerous, the man Zach was most eager to slay.

Pines were only twenty yards off. Smiling at having thwarted his adversaries, Zach angled toward a gap in the tree line. The next moment two more rifles blasted. He felt the horse shudder to the impact of at least one of the balls, giving him an instant in which to tense his leg muscles before the animal suddenly pitched headlong to the earth.

Zach leaped clear in the nick of time. He rolled when he landed and rose in a crouch, the squeal of his mount ringing in his ears. The animal thrashed and kicked, gushing scarlet spray, beyond all hope. Some of the whites laughed and hollered. They believed they had Zach now, that he was as good as caught, as good as dead. He would prove them wrong.

Dashing for the vegetation, Zach reached it as several more rifles boomed. Johnson must have been one of them, because a ball nearly scorched Zach's ear. He flung himself under a pine, flipped to the right, and ran deeper into the undergrowth before the greenhorns could take another bead.

Zach was unarmed, but that didn't deter him. In the heat of combat a warrior often had to make do with what was available. Already Zach was on the lookout for a certain type of rock and long, straight limbs. The stone he needed seemed to leap up at him. It was about seven inches long, triangular in shape, with a rough, serrated edge.

Now Zach needed a limb. But he was still searching when the crash of brush heralded the whites.

"Spread out! Keep your eyes peeled! The nit can't have gotten far!" Vince Kendrick bellowed.

Zach's blood boiled. Kendrick was the kind of white he'd always despised, the kind who hated for hatred's sake, the kind who thought all Indians were beneath contempt. To a fiend like Kendrick, Indians were less than human. Less than wild beasts. They were vermin, to be exterminated as whites saw fit. It was men like Kendrick who ensured the red race and the white race could never live in peace.

Darting behind a bole, Zach marked the positions of the horsemen. Two were off to the right, three to the left. Kendrick and Johnson were in the middle.

"Shoot to kill!" the former commanded. "I don't care if his father has been shadowing us. We'll kill the father, too, when the time comes."

Ed Stark tittered. "I was hoping to have some fun first. Maybe poke out his eyes, chop off his fingers and toes. I love it when they beg for mercy."

"Pay attention to what you're doing, damn you," Kendrick said. "Even nits can bite. He might be unarmed, but that doesn't make him any less dangerous."

For once the hatemonger was right. Zach turned and ran low to the ground, taking advantage of all available cover. He couldn't hope to outrun horses, but if he could stay ahead of them long enough to find a hiding place, the whites were in for a nasty surprise.

Unfortunately, the cover wasn't as thick as Zach had hoped. Some of the brush was dense, but not dense enough to hide him should any of the greenhorns pass within a dozen feet of where he lay.

The whites were conducting a thorough search. Ira Sanders was well to the north, Frank Batson well to the south, so Zach couldn't outflank them. Spaced as they were, about thirty feet apart, Zach couldn't try to slip between them, either.

Circling a cluster of trees, Zach came to a depression about eight feet long and two feet wide. Long ago a tree had fallen and had lain there for years, until time, the elements, and rot had reduced it to splintered fragments.

The soil underneath had settled under its weight, leaving a depression a foot deep. Which wasn't as deep as Zach would like, but it would have to do.

Bending, he quickly scooped out the debris and piled it at the edge. Then he slid in, on his side, and swiftly pulled the pieces of wood and bark over him. There wasn't enough to cover him completely. The largest piece went over his midsection. A small piece of bark he balanced on his cheek, leaving enough space to peer out.

No sooner was Zach done than a rider appeared. It was Elden Johnson, and he was poking into every clump of high weeds, every and all tangled growth.

Zach held his breath. The human anvil's gaze drifted toward the depression. Zach swore he could feel the force of those dark eyes as they swept over him, and it took all his willpower not to leap up and bolt.

Johnson's gaze shifted to the north. He was not quite abreast of the hole and fifteen feet from it when he twisted and scanned the ground around it. His features grew intent, his forehead bunched.

Zach could tell the man suspected something was not as it should be, and it was equally obvious Johnson couldn't figure out exactly what was out of place. Suddenly Johnson focused on one spot, his saddle creaking as he leaned farther down.

Zach had been careful not to leave footprints, but he couldn't completely avoid bending blades of grass and weeds. Had the man noticed some bent stems? Maybe the partial smudge of a heel print? Grasping the stone, Zach prepared to rush Frazier's killer. It wasn't much of a weapon, but it was sharp enough to pierce flesh. A blow to the throat or the eye should do the job if Johnson didn't shoot him first.

The marksman moved closer. Just when Zach was on the verge of bursting upward and attacking him, Ed Stark called out.

"Hey! Over here! I think I've found something!"

Elden Johnson straightened and trotted off. Everyone other than the flankers bustled to where the rat-faced man knelt and climbed down to inspect what he had discovered.

Zach raised himself up high enough to watch.

"See? It's a footprint, as sure as I'm breathing," Stark declared. "The 'breed is heading that way." He pointed to the northeast.

Vince Kendrick took one look and cuffed the smaller man on the back of the head. "You idiot. It's a bear print. I'm no tracker, but even I can tell that." Stooping, he touched the ground. "See here? The outline of its claws?"

"The track is five or six days old," Ira Sanders said. "That's why the claw marks aren't very clear."

"Sorry," Stark said sheepishly. "How was I to know?"

"You could use your pitiful excuse for a brain," Kendrick retorted. "The 'breed has gained ground on us, thanks to you. From now on don't holler unless you're absolutely sure you've found something."

"Don't holler at all," Elden Johnson amended. "It will give away where we are. If any of you find sign, flap your arms."

"Good idea," Kendrick said.

Again they spread out, again they advanced. Johnson rode on with the rest. Soon they were out of sight, and Zach sprang erect, scattering the wood and bark. He roamed among the pines, scouring the carpet of pine needles for a downed limb that would suit his purpose. A live limb would be too supple, too hard to break off. What he needed was one that had been dead awhile, that had hardened and could be trimmed. He found a branch he thought was right, but when he tried to sharpen it, the end shattered.

Zach never gave any thought to fleeing. He could have. There was no one to stop him. But running would be an admission the whites had beaten him. They would live. They would go back up the mountain and help themselves to all the gold they could carry.

They might even find Ben Frazier's cache. So rank an injustice must never come to pass!

For long minutes Zach hunted. Two other branches proved to have flaws. He wondered if he would ever locate a suitable one, and then there it was, over five feet long with little to trim off.

Kneeling, Zach set to work. The stone was crude, but it worked. After the offshoots were stripped, he sawed at the end, peeling thin strips until his makeshift lance was ready. Then he hefted it, testing the balance.

The greenhorns were well to the east. Zach trailed them; the hunted had become the hunter. He needed a rifle and an ammo pouch and powder horn, and then he would show them why even the mighty Sioux respected the prowess of the Shoshones.

Quiet shrouded the woods. Unnatural quiet, as when predators were on the prowl. Or humans were abroad.

To gauge how far ahead the whites were, Zach lowered onto his stomach and pressed an ear to the ground, a trick his Shoshone grandfather had taught him. The earth carried sound quite well. Faintly, but distinctly, Zach heard the muted drum of heavy hooves, a *clomp-clomp-clomp* like the slow beat of a tom-tom.

Zach began to rise, then placed his ear to the ground again. Were his ears deceiving him, or did some of the sounds come from behind him? That couldn't be, unless several of the whites had circled to the rear without him being aware, which was unlikely. He listened closely but now heard only sounds from in front. Evidently he had been mistaken.

Standing, Zach stalked his foes. He glided rapidly along until movement pegged where Vince Kendrick and Elden Johnson were. The pair were consulting. Zach also spied Cyrus Walton and Ed Stark. He selected the rodent and crept toward him.

Zach knew that once he threw the lance, he must move like a greased rattler. He must arm himself with a rifle before the others stopped him. If he could claim

Stark's horse without it acting up, so much the better.

Zach was halfway to the unsuspecting Stark when something—a premonition, perhaps—compelled him to glance over his shoulder. He was startled to discover a line of riders moving slowly toward him. So he had heard something, after all!

Even more startling was who they were.

The Utes were closing in.

Louisa May Clark's mother once mentioned that the worst experience any woman could ever have was for a man to force himself on her. "It's a vile violation of all we are," Mary Clark had said. "Any man who would do such a thing is the lowest of the low, a brute who deserves to have his manhood hacked off. If anyone ever tries to do that to you, resist with all your being. Even if it means your life. Better to sacrifice yourself than bear a horrid emotional scar for the rest of your days."

Her mother had been so bitter, so vehement, that Lou speculated maybe her mother had been a victim of molestation. But Lou could never bring herself to ask. Some matters were too intensely personal. And she had no real desire to know, anyway.

Lou never forgot those words, though. Especially when the family headed west, and Lou heard scary tales of women who had suffered the proverbial fate worse than death. Such stories were legion, bandied about much as the men spent hours recounting clashes between whites and the red man. Frequently, the accounts had no basis in fact. They were the product of tavern gossip. Yet that didn't stop everyone from endlessly repeating them.

Now, as Bartholomew Dunne hitched at his belt while leering at her as if she were the main course at a banquet, all of Louisa's fear welled up. A tidal wave of fright and loathing and resentment that any man could think to do so horrible a deed to any woman.

Lou was proud of having saved herself for marriage.

It was normal in her day and age for girls to do so. But there were some who surrendered their virtue before being joined in wedlock, and paid a dreadful toll. Her mother had told her that most girls who gave in to temptation wound up walking the streets at night, or paraded their wares in houses of ill repute. Lou had been so scared on hearing it, she'd vowed no male would ever touch her—there—unless it was her husband.

Bartholomew Dunne had other ideas. He was starting to undo his belt buckle. "You'll like this so much, girly, you'll never want me to stop."

Lou responded by drawing her knees to her chest and thrusting both feet at the trapper's shins. That she smashed his legs out from under him surprised her even more than it did him.

As Dunne fell, Lou rolled. She was upright in the blink of an eye and took a bound, but callused fingers closed around her left ankle and she was yanked off balance. She tried to right herself, and had almost succeeded when another hand clamped onto her other leg and down she went.

"Struggle all you want, gal. I like it when they do."

Revulsion lent Lou strength. Tearing a leg free, she kicked him. Once, twice, three times, full in the face, and the third time his lower lip split, spurting crimson. Dunne snarled like a panther and clawed higher, seeking to wrap his arms around her waist. Lou wasn't going to let him. She rammed her heel into his shoulder, into his neck.

"Hold still, damn you!" Dunne hissed.

The man couldn't be serious. Lou was supposed to just lie there while he abused her? Her next kick connected with an ear. Howling, Dunne recoiled, and Lou surged to her knees.

"You rotten bitch!"

A backhand caught Lou across the face. Not hard enough to split her skin or break her teeth, but enough to knock her over. Before she could scramble onto her hands and knees, Bartholomew Dunne was on top of her, ripping at her clothes like a wild beast. But where a beast's razor claws would slice her buckskin shirt apart, Dunne's couldn't do more than tear off a few whangs.

"Enough!" he raged, placing his hands on her shoulders and slamming her flat. "You're slippier than an eel!"

Dunne had no idea how slippery she could really be. Wrenching to the left, Lou drove her knee into his stomach. The would-be rapist gurgled and folded like a book. She pushed out from under, rose, and ran like a panicked doe.

"Stop, or I'll shoot!"

Lou would rather be slain than ravaged. She looked back and saw him leveling a flintlock. Or trying to, for he couldn't quite hold it steady.

"I meant it!" was Dunne's final warning.

Cutting to the left, Lou was a footstep ahead of the lead that sought her heart. She ran faster, winding like a doe among the trees, until her lungs were fit to explode. Heaving for breath, she slowed, a deep pain in her ribs compounding the torment. She had done it, though! She had given him the slip and now all she need do was stay shy of him until he tired of hunting for her and wandered elsewhere.

Lou sank to her knees, holding her side.

Brittle brush crackled. Dunne was after her, blundering from growth to growth like a bull that had drunk tainted water. He cursed nonstop, more swearwords in one minute than Lou had heard her pa say in all the years he lived.

"I'll get you!" Dunne panted. "If it takes the rest of the day, I'm not quitting until you're mine!"

Lou didn't have that long. Stalking Coyote needed her. Somehow she must slink off, obtain a horse, and ride like a chinook wind to her betrothed's aid.

"Make it easy on yourself, girly! The longer I have to look, the more you'll regret it! Where are you?"

153

The man had been in the mountains too long. He thought everyone was as stupid as he was. Lou spotted his legs moving past a small tree, so she rose and staggered off, gaining energy with every step. Unbidden tears dampened her eyes and she blinked them away. She refused to be weak. She refused to give in to despair.

It dawned on her that Dunne had fallen silent. Halting, she cocked her head but couldn't hear him blundering about. Why not?

There could be only one answer.

The lecher was doing the same thing she was! Louisa stood stock-still, hoping to wait him out. He was bound to be impatient and would move before she did. But the seconds became a minute and the minutes followed one after another until over five had gone by and she hadn't heard so much as a leaf rustle.

Where was he? Worried, now, that he knew where she was and he was creeping toward her, Lou rotated a full three hundred and sixty degrees. Her anxiety climbed, and she beat down an urge to run pell-mell in any direction. She must be calm. She mustn't lost control. She could beat him if she didn't lose her head.

Like a tiny mouse slinking from a ravenous cat, Lou tiptoed to the southeast. She prayed the dun hadn't strayed, prayed for once luck would favor her.

The patter of onrushing feet proved to the contrary. A savage whoop of exultation sent a shiver down her spine as Lou spun. Bartholomew Dunne was almost upon her, his arms outflung, demonic joy lighting his craggy features. He tackled her. Against someone his size and weight she was helpless to resist.

Smashed to the earth, Lou nearly blacked out. Her wrists were seized. When her vision cleared, she was staring up into the contorted mask of a satyr. He laughed, wriggled his knees on her chest, and lowered his mouth close to hers.

"Comfortable, girly?"

Lou attempted to bite him, but Dunne pulled back.

"No you don't! For such a small fry, you sure are feisty."

"Do this, and so help me I'll kill you."

"When I'm done you'll be in no shape to lift a finger, let alone harm anyone," Dunne gloated. Puckering his lips, he rimmed them with his tongue. "I've never had one as young as you. And I hear the younger they are, the sweeter they taste. What say I find out?"

Lou desperately jerked her face away, but Dunne chortled and tried to mold his mouth to hers. *"No!"* she screamed, fear eclipsing all else. She bucked and heaved, but she couldn't gain enough leverage to throw him off. "No! No! No!"

Bartholomew Dunne's face was a whisker's width from her own. Abruptly, he pulled back and shot to his feet.

Then Lou saw that he hadn't risen on his own. Someone had *hauled* him off her and was holding him as she might hold a doll. Her heart swelled. Speechless with disbelief, she was convinced she must be dreaming.

But it was real.

"What the hell—?" Dunne blurted, and turned to gape at the much bigger man who held him, a wide-shouldered mountain of muscle whose bearded face was terrible to behold. "Let go of me, you bastard."

The newcomer made no answer. His left hand was locked on Dunne's shoulder. Now his right hand flashed, wrapped around Dunne's wrist, and commenced to bend the wrist backward as lesser men might bend a twig.

Dunne shrieked. He sought to break loose, but his strength paled in comparison to that of the other. Inexorably, his wrist kept bending, bending, bending, until the whole arm was at an unnatural angle. Something had to give, and it did. The *crack* of bone was as loud as a gunshot.

Wailing, Dunne flapped like a stricken raven. Without ceremony he was flung to the earth. A foot crashed into his ribs, and again the snap of bone was ghastly clear. He howled and convulsed as if having a fit.

Louisa's rescuer gazed down at her. "He can't be allowed to hurt anyone ever again. Do you understand?"

At a loss for words, Lou nodded.

"Please, please!" Dunne mewed. His appeal was wasted. Immensely strong hands gripped him by the front of his shirt and effortlessly lifted him. One hand closed on his neck, one took firm hold of his jaw. Comprehension left Dunne momentarily horror-struck. Then he rained his fists in a frenzy.

The man began to twist Dunne's neck in one direction—and Dunne's jaw in the other.

Lou was riveted to the spectacle. She felt no sympathy for her molester, none whatsoever.

Spittle flecked Bartholomew Dunne's lips and chin as he fought maniacally for his life. Wheezing like a steam engine about to rupture, he punched and kicked, but he might as well have hit solid marble for all the effect it had. His arms gradually weakened. Whining pathetically, he pried at the bigger man's hands with his fingernails. *"Who are you?"* he managed to shriek.

The mountain man paused. The look he bestowed on Louisa was filled with the same love her own father had shown her. "I'm Nate King. This young lady is going to marry my son. That makes her my daughter." And at that, Nate twisted his arms in a tremendous, grinding wrench.

Bartholomew Dunne's body plopped beside Lou. She started to rise but was too weak. An arm as stout as a redwood lifted her, and she collapsed against her rescuer's broad chest. The tears she had resisted now flowed freely. Once unleashed, she cried and cried and cried. At length, wiping her face with her sleeve, she straightened and kissed him on the cheek.

"Thank you."

"What else is family for?"

The tears poured anew. Nate King tenderly guided Lou from the grisly scene, saying, "Let's go find my son."

Chapter Twelve

The Ute war party numbered over fifteen strong. The warriors had painted faces and had painted their war-horses, and every man bristled with weapons. They had bows, lances, war clubs, and knives, but no guns. Rifles and pistols were hard for Indians to come by. In the old days friendly tribes could trade beaver plews for them, but now that the beaver trade was dying out, the Indians had little to offer that white traders rated worth the value of a firearm. As for hostile tribes, the only way they could get their hands on guns was to strip them from the cold fingers of dead gun owners.

This war party had bided its time, stalking the greenhorns until ready to engage their enemy. Why they had picked this particular moment was a question only they could answer.

Zachary King was caught in the middle, pinned between two opposing forces, either of whom would gladly rub him out. The Utes hadn't spotted him yet. Kendrick's outfit were unaware the war party was stalking them; the whites were too intent on their search for him.

Crouched behind a tree trunk, Zachary glanced from one group to the other and back again. To try and break through the Ute line would result in certain death. There were too many, and they were too alert. He might be able to slip away and sneak around ahead of the whites, but that would take time, time he didn't have. The Utes were bound to attack soon.

Zach must do *something*. To just wait there invited discovery. He scanned the brush, the grass, the trees, seeking a place to hide.

The snap of a branch brought Zach's head around. *One of the whites was coming back!* It was Elden Johnson. Maybe the marksman had remembered whatever he saw near the hole and was returning to investigate. Or maybe Kendrick had sent him to make another sweep of the immediate area. Whatever the case, it changed everything.

Flattening, his makeshift lance at his side, Zach waited for the thunderclap that would trigger a storm of violence. He saw Johnson glued to the ground, checking for sign. He saw the Utes spot Johnson, and stop. A second later Elden Johnson lifted his head and set eyes on them.

The tableau froze. Neither the Utes nor Johnson moved. They took the measure of one another, and to Johnson's credit, he displayed no fear.

Then a young warrior on the left raised a bow with an arrow already notched to the sinew string. Elden Johnson, whipping up his rifle, put a ball through the man's forehead. As one, the rest of the warriors vented war cries and charged.

"The Utes! The Utes are on us!" Johnson shouted, wheeling his mount and speeding toward his companions.

Zach hugged the ground. The line of Utes thundered down on him, and suddenly they were on both sides, some so close he could have jabbed his lance into their mounts. He thought for sure that one of them would see him, but none did. They were staring straight ahead, at their quarry.

Zach didn't delay. As soon as the Utes swept past him, he was on his feet and running. He had to get as far from there as he could, and fast. But he had gone less than a dozen steps when he saw *more* warriors, a second line with almost as many warriors as the first. Diving under a small pine, he eluded detection. Temporarily, at least.

The second line, Zach realized, was to prevent any whites from fleeing to the west. And in that case, there must be even more Utes to the north, south, and east. The war party had laid a clever trap.

Only, now Zach was caught in it, too!

Deeper in the forest bedlam broke out. Rifles blasted in a ragged volley. Curses and war whoops mixed with the whinnies of horses and the crash of undergrowth to attest to the fury of the clash.

Zach could imagine it in his mind's eye.

The initial volley would break the Ute charge and the warriors would veer off to regroup. Kendrick's men would bunch up for mutual protection, frantically reloading and debating what to do. They would decide to flee to the east and encounter another line of warriors.

A smattering of shots hinted Zach was right.

Next the whites would wheel to the south or north and fly for their lives. Again they would be blocked by waiting warriors. Now they realized they were in a trap. Now they knew they were completely surrounded. They would stop and reload again, and one of them, probably Elden Johnson, would say that the only way they were going to get out of there alive was to mount a charge of their own and break through the ring of Utes. Exactly where they would try, Zach couldn't guess.

"Give 'em hell, boys!" Vince Kendrick roared.

Guns banged, rifles first and then pistols. Once more the crackle of bushes and weeds betokened the rush of horses. A man screamed. A strident nicker pealed.

Zach saw the greenhorns galloping toward him in a knot, firing just as rapidly as they could reload. Kendrick was in the lead, and he had a bloody gash on his temple. Billy Batson was worse off, with an arrow jutting from a shoulder. Of his brother, Frank, there was no sign, although Frank's horse was with the rest, running on its own.

A burly Ute popped out of thin air, a lance upraised to throw. Elden Johnson instantly sent a pistol ball into the warrior's chest.

A glittering arrow streaked true, embedding itself in Cyrus Walton's thigh. The former clerk screeched and grabbed it, which only made his agony worse. He started to fall behind the others but quickly caught up.

Zach decided to stay right where he was. The whites would sweep past him and the Utes would follow them, leaving him all alone and safe. But it was not meant to be. For just then one of the warriors in the second line pointed at the small pine, hiked a war club, and barreled toward him.

What happened next happened so fast, Zach had no time to think. He merely acted and reacted, relying on his reflexes and the oldest of human instincts: self-preservation.

As the young warrior flew forward, Zach sprang to his feet and flung back his right arm. His lance cleaved the air a fraction of a second before the Ute's. The two weapons were twin streaks. The warrior missed Zach's head by the span of his hand. Zach's lance, though, struck the young Ute in the chest, tumbling him in a heap.

Other warriors moved to finish what their fallen friend had started.

It was at that juncture the greenhorns galloped past, and with them the riderless horse belonging to Frank Batson.

The empty saddle was Zach's only hope. Flinging himself at it, he leaped. A slender shaft shot in front of his eyes, another whistled overhead. For a harrowing second he thought he had misjudged and would miss, but his hands found purchase on the pommel and he clung on for dear life.

The Utes were converging to stop the whites. But Kendrick's men were not to be denied. Yet another volley blistered the warriors, a hail of lead dropping four or five in the center. Into the gap poured the greenhorns, and on out of the forest.

A horde of incensed avengers streamed from all four points of the compass. The cry had gone out! The white men were escaping!

Zach was bouncing and swaying uncontrollably, his shoulders under tremendous strain. He sought to clamber up but couldn't hook his leg high enough. Worse, his fingers were losing their grip. To fall would seal his doom. The Utes would be on him before he could stand. He thought of Lou, of how much he looked forward to being her husband, to having her snuggle beside him night after night for the rest of his life, and an extra surge of vitality filled him. With a powerful upward heave, he forked his foot over the horse's back and pulled himself on.

The whites were heading for Gold Mountain. A blunder on their part, Zach figured, since the slopes were so open, so devoid of good cover. But on second thought, he realized it could work in their favor. The Utes wouldn't be able to approach unseen. A small force could hold off a large one indefinitely—or as long as their food, water, and ammo lasted.

Only Cyrus Walton had noticed the addition to their band, and he made no attempt to harm Zach. The arrow in his thigh preoccupied him.

Firing at random as more and more Utes emerged from the trees, the greenhorns held the war party at bay. Zach noticed, though, that the warriors didn't make a determined effort to overtake them. The Utes seemed content to simply follow, just out of rifle range, their numbers swelling until there were over fifty.

So that was why the war party had put off the attack for so long, Zach reflected. They had been waiting for more to arrive.

Vince Kendrick didn't slow until his men were on the lowest slope of Gold Mountain. By then their mounts were lathered with sweat. Kendrick drew rein and shook a fist at the Utes, who were holding to a walk. "Damned savages! Come and get us, if you dare!"

No one appreciated the false bravado, least of all Billy Batson and Cyrus Walton, both of whom were hurting. Billy was the worst, so woozy from loss of blood he could barely stay in the saddle.

Ira Sanders, mopping his brow, chanced to look at Zach. "The rotten 'breed! What's he doing here!" The scarecrow started to bring up his rifle.

A swat of Elden Johnson's Kentucky foiled Sanders. "No," he said sternly. "Don't kill him."

"Why the hell not?" Sanders demanded.

Kendrick was just as perplexed. "What's gotten into you? We were going to kill him anyway, remember? Why not finish him now?"

Zach disliked how they talked about him as if he weren't even there—or beneath their contempt.

Johnson busied himself reloading. "The 'breed's in the same boat we are. The Utes are as much his enemies as they are ours. So he'll help us fight. And since we're outnumbered ten to one, we can use all the help we can get."

Kendrick, Sanders, and Ed Stark weren't pleased, but they didn't argue. "I'd sooner trust a griz than a half-breed," Ed Stark said.

"Give him one of Billy's pistols," Johnson said. "You're closest."

"Like hell I will!" Stark responded. "He's liable to turn it on me and blow my brains out."

"And I'm telling you he won't," Johnson said.

"No, I won't," Zach spoke on his own behalf. It rankled him to have Ben Frazier's killer as an ally, but there it was. "Those Utes want my hair just as much as they want yours. Like your friend just said, I'm stuck helping you whether I want to or not."

Ed Stark was still suspicious. "I don't know—"

"Do it," Vince Kendrick said, ending the debate.

Billy Batson never objected as Stark stripped him of a pistol, his ammo pouch, and his powder horn. The young farmer was barely conscious, the front of his shirt drenched bright scarlet.

"What are those devils waiting for?" Ira Sanders asked. "Why don't they do something?"

The Utes had halted well out on the flatland. Wounded were being tended, water skins passed around.

"They're in no hurry," Zach said. "They'll finish us off whenever they want. But without losing many of their own, if they can."

Elden Johnson nodded. "The boy's right. Indians never throw their lives away if they can help it."

Cyrus Walton was groaning and gritting his teeth. "I say we light a shuck while the getting is good. We'll ride north until we've lost them, then swing east and not stop until we reach the Mississippi."

Vince Kendrick nipped that idea in the bud. "We wouldn't get two miles, the shape our horses are in. No, we'll hole up until dark to give the critters some rest, then try and slip away."

"Not me," Walton said, reining his mount around. "Don't anyone try to stop me, either," he warned. A flick of his reins sent his horse into a trot.

"The fool," Elden Johnson said.

The Utes sat and watched the pudgy man leave. Not until he was several hundred yards distant did ten warriors detach themselves from the main group and trail him at a leisurely pace.

Ira Sanders motioned. "He'll never get away.

Maybe we should go after him. Fetch him back even if he refuses.''

"Forget about Cy," Kendrick barked. "He made his bed, now he can lie in it. We have ourselves to think of. Come on.''

Sanders was the only one who hesitated when the others hurried on up the mountain. Zach also hung back, but only to verify the pistol was loaded. As he wedged it under his belt, Ira Sanders regarded him intently.

"We're all going to die, aren't we?"

No answer was called for. The scarecrow spurred his horse, and Zach fell into step in his wake. Their deaths were a foregone conclusion. All they could do was die with dignity. Zach would go down fighting, as a Shoshone warrior should, taking as many of his enemies with him as he could.

Dying didn't worry Zach nearly as much as Louisa did. She was out there, somewhere. Maybe close by. He shuddered to think of her fate should the Utes get their hands on her. Hopefully, she'd gone to get help, to bring his pa. His father would track the greenhorns clear to Gold Mountain and find his body. So there was some consolation in knowing his parents wouldn't spend the rest of their lives wondering about his fate. As for Lou, Zach hoped his folks would take her in and treat her as one of their own.

Vince Kendrick halted again when his tattered brigade reached the shelf partway up the mountain. Open slopes above and below made it an ideal spot for them to make their stand. After tying their mounts to the few pines, the whites moved to the rim. Except for Billy, who collapsed against a boulder.

"What the hell are those Injuns up to now?" Ed Stark asked.

Two groups of half a dozen warriors each were going in opposite directions, one around the base of the mountain to the north, the other to the south.

"They're going to circle around," Elden Johnson

said. "Close the back door so we can't sneak away."

"Now look," Stark declared.

A council was being held. While several warriors stood guard over the warhorses and others rested, half a dozen leaders had formed a circle and were seated cross-legged.

Zach had a hunch why. Few whites were aware of how highly independent Indians were. Most were loath to bow to any authority. Tribal leaders, while highly respected, did not have the right to boss members of the tribe around. Their word wasn't law, as the whites might say. Any warrior was free to do as he chose when a leader's wishes conflicted with his own. The circle below hinted at a difference of opinion the Utes must smooth over before the war party committed itself to a course of action. It would buy the whites a few extra hours of life.

Zach, too. Hunkering, he rested his elbows on his knees and gazed at the mantle of snow covering far off Longs Peak. To the north of it was the family's cabin. He prayed Louisa reached them safely.

"Where'd those buzzards come from?" Ira Sanders wanted to know.

Four of the ungainly birds were wheeling above boulders lower down. The scarecrow had forgotten about Ben Frazier and Bessy.

Vince Kendrick announced, "When it's dark enough, we'll make a break for it. They can't be everywhere at once. Some of us are bound to get through. We'll meet up again at Bent's Fort."

"We do have a chance," Ed Stark said, trying to convince himself more than the others. "There's only thirty or so of those scum down there now. Once we slip past them, they'll never catch us."

Elden Johnson walked over to Zach. "What about you, boy? Do you reckon we can make it out alive?"

"It can be done."

"How would you go about it?"

Zach had been giving escape some thought. "I

would spook the horses. While the Utes chased them, I'd head for the trees.''

Ed Stark snorted in disgust. ''Stupidest idea I've ever heard. Only an idiot would try to get away on foot. They'd run you down and use you to bloody their lances.''

''It might work,'' Johnson disagreed, ''if we timed it right, and if they didn't catch on that no one was on the horses.''

''You can go along with his loco stunt if you want, but not me,'' Ed Stark said. ''I'm not letting my horse out of my sight.''

Zach rose. ''It doesn't matter what you think. We'll never get to try. The Utes will attack before the sun goes down, so they don't lose the light. They'll come from below and above and maybe both sides, all at once.''

Ira Sanders's Adam's apple bobbed. ''Sweet Jesus! We'll be massacred!''

''We've already lost one more,'' Elden Johnson said, pointing.

Billy Batson, the young man from Ohio who had hankered to buy his pa a new plow more than anything else in the world, would never buy anyone anything ever again. He had slumped on his side, his blank expression as empty as his pockets of the gold he had thought would be the answer to all his prayers.

No one tried to stop Zach when he helped himself to Billy's other flintlock. There was no rifle; Batson had lost it down in the trees.

The whites were quiet now, each lost in thought. Stark and Sanders were bundles of raw nerves. Neither could stand still for more than a few seconds. They paced like caged cougars, Stark gnawing on his nails.

Kendrick never took his eyes off the Utes except to scour the slopes above. Fueled by his hatred, he was more angry than fearful.

Only Elden Johnson did not show any emotion. As composed as ever, he stood aloof from the others. No one disturbed him until Zach made bold to go over. Something needed to be aired.

"If not for the Utes, I'd kill you myself."

"You would try, boy."

"You shot my friend."

"I almost shot you, too. Vince wanted both of you dead."

"And you always do what Kendrick says, is that it?"

"Yes."

"Why?"

Johnson looked up. "He's my friend."

"That's the only reason?"

"It's enough."

As the sun dipped lower and lower, the tension on the shelf became thick enough to cut with a Green River knife.

The face of Gold Mountain underwent a sinister change. Low down the shadows lengthened, spreading like a plague of locusts, devouring all in their path. Yet on the shelf, and higher up, daylight hadn't faded. Anyone who stepped near the edge was silhouetted against the sky.

The Utes stirred, taking up their weapons and preparing for battle. They fanned out in a crescent moon a hundred yards from tip to tip. Then they climbed, darting from boulder to boulder with the agility of mountain goats.

"Dying time is here," Elden Johnson said gravely, taking up his rifle.

"And it's too light to run off the horses," Vince Kendrick said. "They're doing just like the 'breed said they would. Well, let's give the bastards hell, boys. We'll keep them pinned down until dark."

The whites formed in a short skirmish line. At a word from their leader, they fired a volley that caught several members of the war party by surprise. Ed Stark and Ira Sanders cheered when the Utes fell, but it was a hollow, fleeting triumph. From then on the warriors rarely showed themselves. And each time one did briefly appear, it was closer to the shelf.

"They'll be in among us before we know it," Ed Stark said. "God, I don't want to die!"

Hardly had the words been uttered when a loud whizzing was heard and the feathered end of an arrow blossomed between Ed Stark's shoulder blades. Stark half rose, half turned, amazement lining his features. His lips moved like those of a fish out of water, then he tottered toward Kendrick, declared, "I'll be damned!" Just like that he keeled over, dead before he stopped moving.

The three other whites whirled and sought targets higher up, but there were none. Zach, farther back from the edge, need not worry. Yet.

Ira Sanders was in the grip of rampant fright. "We can't stay here, Vince! They'll pick us off one at a time! I want a fighting chance."

"All we have to do is hold out until sunset," Kendrick reiterated.

"We don't have that long!" Sanders sprinted to the horses, untied his, and forked the saddle. He saw neither Kendrick nor Johnson had moved. "What's gotten into you two? Do you *want* to die!"

Elden Johnson was on his stomach, sighting down his barrel. "You won't get thirty feet, Ira. It's best if you stick with us."

"Not on your life! Look me up in St. Louis if you live!" Sanders went over the crest at a gallop, angling to the northwest.

Zach ran to the rim to see how far the scarecrow got. It wasn't far at all. Not even thirty feet. Shafts rained down, piercing Sanders again and again. He never got off a shot, his rifle landing beside him in the dirt.

Warriors rushed to claim both the horse and the dead man's weapons. In doing so they exposed themselves to Kendrick and Johnson, who wounded two. But that did not stop the rest. To the Utes, a rifle was a prize worth any cost. Seven broke cover, eager to be the one to own it.

"Kill them!" Vince Kendrick snarled. "Kill them all!"

It was then, with the attention of the Utes diverted, that Zach went over the rim himself. But on foot, low to the ground, and to the southeast. Kendrick and Johnson were so busy picking off warriors, they never saw him leave.

A gully cloaked in shadow was Zach's goal. From there he could work his way lower in relative safety. Could he reach it? Or would he end up like Sanders? As if in answer, an arrow sprouted in the earth on his right. Another did likewise on his left.

Zach zigzagged, bounding like an antelope. Arrows fell fast and furious, some missing him by inches. Off to the left a warrior yelled.

Only fifteen feet remained when Zach slipped on the steep slope. He crashed onto his back, his momentum carrying him almost to the gully. Scrambling onto his hands and knees, he was shocked when a familiar broad-shouldered figure reared up, grabbed hold of him, and bodily heaved him over the side. In a spray of dust and dirt Zach came to a stop—and there were his dun and the mare and the most beautiful girl in the world, beaming at him with tears of pure joy in her eyes.

"Pa! Lou!"

"Mount and ride!" Nate King directed.

The trio swept down the gully and disappeared around a bend. Up on the shelf only one rifle still boomed, amid a bloodthirsty chorus of war whoops.

Another hour, and the mountain lay peaceful and still under twinkling stars. The three people who raced into the night were safe. And, at that particular moment, they were three of the happiest souls alive.

WILDERNESS

#24

Mountain Madness

⟵————————⟶

David Thompson

When Nate King comes upon a pair of green would-be trappers from New York, he is only too glad to risk his life to save them from a Piegan war party. It is only after he takes them into his own cabin that he realizes they will repay his kindness...with betrayal. When the backshooters reveal their true colors, Nate knows he is in for a brutal battle—with the lives of his family hanging in the balance.

___4399-8 $3.99 US/$4.99 CAN

Dorchester Publishing Co., Inc.
P.O. Box 6640
Wayne, PA 19087-8640

Please add $1.75 for shipping and handling for the first book and $.50 for each book thereafter. NY, NYC, and PA residents, please add appropriate sales tax. No cash, stamps, or C.O.D.s. All orders shipped within 6 weeks via postal service book rate. Canadian orders require $2.00 extra postage and must be paid in U.S. dollars through a U.S. banking facility.

Name_____
Address_____
City_____ State_____ Zip_____
I have enclosed $_____ in payment for the checked book(s).
Payment <u>must</u> accompany all orders. ❑ Please send a free catalog.
CHECK OUT OUR WEBSITE! www.dorchesterpub.com

 **David Thompson**

Follow the adventures of mountain man Nate King, as he struggles to survive in America's untamed West.

Wilderness #20: Wolf Pack. Nathaniel King is forever on the lookout for possible dangers, and he is always ready to match death with death. But when a marauding band of killers and thieves kidnaps his wife and children, Nate has finally run into enemies who push his skill and cunning to the limit. And it will only take one wrong move for him to lose his family—and his only reason for living.

___3729-7 $3.99 US/$4.99 CAN

Wilderness #21: Black Powder. In the great unsettled Rocky Mountains, a man has to struggle every waking hour to scratch a home from the land. When mountain man Nathaniel King and his family are threatened by a band of bloodthirsty slavers, they face enemies like none they've ever battled. But the sun hasn't risen on the day when the mighty Nate King will let his kin be taken captive without a fight to the death.

___3820-X $3.99 US/$4.99 CAN

Wilderness #22: Trail's End. In the savage Rockies, trouble is always brewing. Strong mountain men like Nate King risk everything to carve a new world from the frontier, and they aren't about to give it up without a fight. But when some friendly Crows ask Nate to help them rescue a missing girl from a band of murderous Lakota, he sets off on a journey that will take him to the end of the trail—and possibly the end of his life.

3849-8 $3.99 US/$4.99 CAN

Dorchester Publishing Co., Inc.
P.O. Box 6640
Wayne, PA 19087-8640

Please add $1.75 for shipping and handling for the first book and $.50 for each book thereafter. NY, NYC, and PA residents, please add appropriate sales tax. No cash, stamps, or C.O.D.s. All orders shipped within 6 weeks via postal service book rate. Canadian orders require $2.00 extra postage and must be paid in U.S. dollars through a U.S. banking facility.

Name_____
Address_____
City_____ State_____ Zip_____
I have enclosed $_____ in payment for the checked book(s).
Payment <u>must</u> accompany all orders. ❏ Please send a free catalog.

WILDERNESS
The epic struggle for survival in America's untamed West.

#17: Trapper's Blood. In the wild Rockies, any man who dares to challenge the brutal land has to act as judge, jury, and executioner against his enemies. And when trappers start turning up dead, their bodies horribly mutilated, Nate and his friends vow to hunt down the merciless killers. Taking the law into their own hands, they soon find that one hasty decision can make them as guilty as the murderers they want to stop.

__3566-9 $3.50 US/$4.50 CAN

#16: Blood Truce. Under constant threat of Indian attack, a handful of white trappers and traders live short, violent lives, painfully aware that their next breath could be their last. So when a deadly dispute between rival Indian tribes explodes into a bloody war, Nate has to make peace between enemies—or he and his young family will be the first to lose their scalps.

__3525-1 $3.50 US/$4.50 CAN

#15: Winterkill. Any greenhorn unlucky enough to get stranded in a wilderness blizzard faces a brutal death. But when Nate takes in a pair of strangers who have lost their way in the snow, his kindness is repaid with vile treachery. If King isn't careful, he and his young family will not live to see another spring.

__3487-5 $3.50 US/$4.50 CAN

Dorchester Publishing Co., Inc.
P.O. Box 6640
Wayne, PA 19087-8640

Please add $1.75 for shipping and handling for the first book an $.50 for each book thereafter. NY, NYC, and PA resident please add appropriate sales tax. No cash, stamps, or C.O.D.s. A orders shipped within 6 weeks via postal service book rate.
Canadian orders require $2.00 extra postage and must be paid in U.S. dollars through a U.S. banking facility.

Name_____

Address_____

City_____ State_____ Zip_____

I have enclosed $_____ in payment for the checked book(s)

Payment __must__ accompany all orders. ☐ Please send a free catalog

WILDERNESS

VENGEANCE TRAIL
DEATH HUNT

The epic struggle for survival in America's untamed West.

Vengeance Trail. When Nate and his mentor, Shakespeare McNair, make enemies of two Flathead Indians, their survival skills are tested as never before.

And in the same action-packed volume....

Death Hunt. Upon the birth of their first child, Nathaniel King and his wife are overjoyed. But their delight turns to terror when Nate accompanies the men of Winona's tribe on a deadly buffalo hunt. If King doesn't return, his family is sure to perish.

___4297-5 $4.99 US/$5.99 CAN

Dorchester Publishing Co., Inc.
P.O. Box 6640
Wayne, PA 19087-8640

Please add $1.75 for shipping and handling for the first book and $.50 for each book thereafter. NY, NYC, and PA residents, please add appropriate sales tax. No cash, stamps, or C.O.D.s. All orders shipped within 6 weeks via postal service book rate. Canadian orders require $2.00 extra postage and must be paid in U.S. dollars through a U.S. banking facility.

Name_____

Address_____

City_____ State_____ Zip_____

I have enclosed $_____ in payment for the checked book(s).

Payment <u>must</u> accompany all orders. ☐ Please send a free catalog.